The Hunger Games Trilogy: A Super Index

by Duncan Scott

copyright 2014

Index of Master Index:

Book 1 - The Hunger Games

1-145

Book 2 - Catching Fire

152-388

Book 3 - Mockingjay

388-end

by Duncan Scott

a	privilege	326
a	remarkable	160
abandoning	96, 542
abandonment	20, 204, 408
abandons	250
abilities	20, 50, 393
abnormally	562
abounds	6
about	what	157
abruptly	426
absconded	534
absences	499
absorbs	322
abused	224, 428, 496
abuses	491
abusing	281
accelerated	525
accents	66, 568
accepting	435, 450, 579
accepts	37, 226, 291
accessories	239, 286
accidentally	170
accidents.	A	95

accompanied	440, 473, 498, 520, 531, 598, 600
accompanies	327, 333
accompanying	196
accomplices	596
accounted	475, 476
accounts	73
accumulated	185, 247
accurately	196
accusations	93, 331, 415
accusingly	153, 365
aches	47, 154, 280, 398
achieved	115, 411, 524
aching	11, 88, 173, 399
acknowledged	280, 400
acknowledging	13, 43, 469
ACKNOWLEDGMENTS	401, 608
acorns	59
acquaintances	568
acquired	577
acted	28, 109, 112, 168, 190, 197, 203, 212, 225, 233, 339, 488
actions	18, 33, 129, 181, 189, 195, 213, 470
activated	119, 534, 539, 550, 552, 581
activates	564
actively	358, 504
activities	7
activity	flurry of 445
acts	352, 362, 606
actually	idea of 157
acutely	234
adapting	499
added	3, 27, 214, 263, 281, 298
addicts	308
adding	187, 229, 256, 281, 369, 370, 378, 544
additions	236, 607
addressed	33, 279, 405, 426
addresses	208, 474
addressing	14, 42, 66, 515
adds	5, 42, 73, 114, 172, 223, 277, 278, 298, 330, 342, 370, 386, 422, 493, 527, 534, 558, 561, 569, 572, 577
adequately	324
adjourned	534
adjourns	442
adjusted	570
adjusting	65, 293, 350, 411, 439, 527
adjusts	184, 189, 193, 283, 304, 357, 550, 595

administered   471
admired   500
admirers   72, 314
admiring   242
admits   44, 52, 293, 497, 499, 504, 517, 530, 574
admitted   490, 592
admitting   460
adores   30, 65, 377
adoring   237
adorned   433
adorns   7
Adrienne Vrettos   608
adults   42, 57, 482
advantages   108, 503
adventures   111
adversaries   43, 50, 79, 335, 382, 492
advises   26
advisor   608
advisors   208, 251
affectations   35
affects   213
affixed   204
affixes   439
afforded   327
Afraid I'm   517
aftereffects   351
afternoon|it   380
afternoon's   470, 527
again| 579
again|the   104
ages   10, 243, 281, 303
aggravating   62, 495
aging   311
Agitated   568
ago| 27
agonies   353
agreeing   73, 207, 261
agrees   71, 237, 299, 301, 366, 488, 510, 527, 540, 578, 602
Ahh   43
ails   89
aimed   119, 403
aiming   397, 453
aimlessly   498
air   lack of   92
Airborne Division   438, 443

aired	457, 512, 573, 590
airpower	503
air's	75, 97, 146, 224, 284, 339, 369, 436
airtime	39, 475
Airtime Assault	425, 457, 460
Airtime Assaults	481
alarmed	20, 131, 474, 561
alarming	103, 106, 353, 391
alcoves	546
alerted	336, 357, 386
alertness	559
alerts	100, 480, 559
alive|	421
alive|seems	289
allayed	495
allegations	492
alleys	201, 268
alliances	85, 106
allotted	19, 230
allowing	12, 168, 184
allows	278, 424, 432, 491, 558
ally|what	151
Alma Coin	406
alterations	223, 228, 326
altered	24, 34, 208, 314, 433, 496, 521, 560, 605
alternates	493
alternating	47, 52, 508, 580
alternatives	218
amazes	63
Amazingly	129, 563
American Copyright Conventions	609
amplifies	514
amuses	88
ancestors	446
and|	75
and|all	177
and|and|one	396
and|I	510, 524
and|Peeta	105
Andrea Davis Pinkney	608
anger surge of	89
angers	336, 432
anger's	524
angles	93, 143, 188, 349
angrily	75, 259, 274, 502

animals 3, 6, 24, 32, 37, 45, 56, 59, 77, 82, 92, 129, 143, 156, 166, 175, 268, 331, 346, 357, 400, 430

animal's 144

ankles 355, 430

anklets 422

Annie 374, 375, 377, 399, 407, 432, 483, 488, 491, 493, 494, 520, 522, 528, 529, 532, 535, 543, 553, 566, 596, 597

Annie Cresta 377, 432, 527

Annie's 378, 379, 432, 519, 521, 528

announced 58, 60, 192, 202, 285, 297, 316, 324, 326, 397, 421, 520, 522

announcers 297

announces 78, 286, 484, 576, 578

announcing 123, 142, 431, 581

annoyed 223, 320, 322

annoys 52

annulling 456

anointed 223

another's 10, 404, 579

answered 73, 238

answering 207, 244

answers 63, 68, 75, 133, 162, 176, 188, 194, 196, 220, 251, 258, 259, 264, 323, 343, 363, 373, 392, 416, 427, 429, 438, 444, 448, 467, 492, 500, 512, 530, 540, 567, 575, 596, 601, 605, 609

anthem's 100, 192

antiaircraft 510, 538

anticipated 170, 246, 303, 328, 534, 545

anticipates 559

anticipating 105, 310, 411, 427, 430, 473, 522

anticlimactic 22

antics 556

antidotes 492

antiseptic cloud of 426

antlers 142

ants 40, 103, 104, 510

anxiously 409, 532

anymore 54, 151, 159, 199, 224, 225, 227, 236, 241, 251, 261, 265, 268, 313, 343, 346, 364, 381, 468, 479, 480, 487, 490, 502, 505, 506, 543, 573, 594, 603, 605

anyone's 124, 230, 275, 510, 559

apartments 557, 559, 568, 577

apartments row of 553

apologetically 221

apologized 56, 235, 442

apothecaries 5

Appalachia 23

appalled 450

appearances	185, 199, 207, 237, 244, 406, 423
appeared	45, 52, 131, 233, 293, 329, 351, 366, 426, 427, 495, 503, 542, 598
appearing	371, 388, 453
appears	11, 34, 36, 38, 41, 76, 83, 102, 119, 125, 147, 151, 169, 181, 183, 186, 187, 191, 241, 242, 245, 247, 254, 263, 270, 277, 283, 304, 318, 332, 335, 339, 348, 350, 359, 360, 378, 387, 434, 443, 451, 455, 472, 476, 477, 484, 499, 518, 531, 535, 555, 596
appetites	10, 491
applauding	459
applications	136
applies	34, 485
appreciated	580
appreciates	602
apprehended	577
Apprehensively	184
approached	400
approaches	76, 408
approaching	38, 81, 85, 119, 336, 368, 462
appropriated	272, 577
approved	268, 283, 330, 427, 524
approving	237, 379, 528
aprons	548
arbitrarily	47
are|around	65
area's	368
arena|blew	414
arena|I'd	438
arena|that	197
arenas	77, 535, 607
arena's	366, 383
Arenas	242
argued	435
argues	243
arguing	418, 530, 532
arguments	539
arises	3, 510
armband	434, 443
armies	576
armload	477
arm's	117, 241, 336
arranged	34, 53, 123, 243, 328, 412, 416, 571
arrangements	594
arranges	234, 235, 485, 529
arranging	185, 194, 218, 226
arrested	185, 262, 432, 545, 577
arrivals	538

arrived   55, 68, 98, 143, 161, 213, 214, 216, 243, 286, 294, 305, 356, 404, 433, 456, 474, 476, 504, 505, 528, 555, 573, 591

arrives   4, 185, 219, 257, 267, 302, 443, 539, 588, 606, 607

arrowheads   28, 565

arrows   3, 27, 48, 49, 55, 79, 97, 102, 103, 105, 108, 117, 119, 122, 128, 129, 131, 142, 147, 149, 166, 171, 176, 177, 201, 211, 224, 268, 318, 319, 322, 337, 339, 357, 358, 359, 369, 376, 377, 385, 393, 404, 418, 439, 443, 452, 453, 518, 539, 563, 565, 579, 583, 588, 603, 605

arrow's   55, 180, 345

Arrows   55

arrows sheath of   102, 337

arrows variety of   439

arsenals   503

arteries   390, 495

artfully   133

articulated   372

as|an   543

ash   carpet of   405

ash   piles of   403

asleep|Hazelle   251

asphyxiation   178

assailants   130

assailant's   254

assassinated   602

assassinating   542, 549

assassination   587

assaulted   448, 582

assemblies   7

assembling   35, 262, 448

assesses   532

assessing   402

assigned   217, 327, 420, 451, 461, 475, 479, 520, 527, 535, 538, 540, 546, 579

Assignment Board   525

assimilating   274

assistants   51

assisting   495

associated   42, 361, 501, 502, 591, 609

assumes   135, 170, 171, 328, 493

assures   262, 384, 513, 532, 552, 578

Atala   51, 314

atrocities   565

attaches   388, 443

attacked   7, 57, 123, 199, 346, 355, 390, 414, 473, 493, 516

attacker   357

attackers   338, 393

attacks   93, 366, 383, 388, 410, 474, 518

attains 482
attempted 284, 340, 493, 497
attempting 178, 403, 404, 473, 547
attempts 14, 68, 295, 380, 416, 463, 493, 507, 555
attendants 243, 297, 309
attended 524
attends 207
attentiveness 350
attracts 202
attributed 49, 535
attributes 175, 472
audience| 171
aunt's 246
Author Copyright 611
authorities 201, 402, 578
authorizing 474
automatically 138, 150, 191, 275, 315, 331, 432, 455, 506, 552
automobiles 116, 575
avalanches 503, 508, 509, 510
avenging 177
avenues 67, 559, 568, 580, 584
averted 213
averting 387
avoided 73, 172, 264
avoiding 97, 197, 241, 266, 365, 604
avoids 46, 267, 325
Avox 42, 47, 56, 61, 64, 74, 76, 87, 184, 185, 186, 270, 310, 311, 324, 335, 399, 457, 473, 501, 545, 558, 587
Avoxes 45, 55, 310, 545, 559, 562
awaited 267
awaiting 104, 193, 395, 571, 587, 593
awaits 177, 214, 303, 425, 499, 554
awakens 572
awakes 366
awards 377
awareness 355, 504
awfulness 311
awkwardly 21, 99, 137, 438, 529
babbles 339
babied 205, 503
babies 124
baby's 359
babysitter 314
back.| 129
back| 250

backfired 232, 294
backfires 497
backfiring 246
backpacks 150, 153, 476
backpedal 250, 582
backups 315
backyard 52
backyards 16, 201
bad height of 224
baffled 287, 327, 576
baffling 372
bag|and 139
bag's 98, 478
baked 28, 141, 205, 215, 269, 271, 280
baker's 17, 21, 23, 25, 27, 37, 70
Bakers 242
bakes 205, 599, 607
balances 175
balancing 200
balconies 67
balding 10
ballads 600
balloons 103
ballrooms 587
Bam 219, 472
bandaged 75, 154, 396, 571, 588
bandages 73, 136, 149, 257, 258, 263, 277, 278, 400, 449, 471, 516, 536, 570, 571, 574
bandaging 570
banged 279, 449, 455
banging 92, 103, 216, 334, 603
banks 132, 166, 167, 503, 516
banned 512
banners 9, 229, 245, 324
barbecued 37
barbed coils of 276
barbs 548
bared 177, 357
bargained 373
barking 547
barks 220, 254, 566
barreling 119, 337
barrels 514
barricaded 472, 584
barricades 585

bars   320

based   273, 280, 383, 391, 420, 438, 590

basements   570

bashing   563

basing   40, 282

baskets   200

bathed   14, 223

bathing   321, 367, 410, 482

bathrooms   475

baths   223, 552, 587

battered   29, 412

batteries   415, 482

battle   heart of   545

battles   324, 439

battling   340, 378, 554

beaches   370

beads   353, 472

beaks   302

beams   40, 62, 456, 475

beans   274

beards   456

bearings   128, 334, 550, 588

bears   3, 28, 174

beasts   357

beats   150, 346, 604

beauticians   428

beauties   486, 589

Beauty Base Zero   433, 434, 594

beauty scent of   74

bcavers   559

Because|because|she   70

beckoned   439

beckons   30

bedrooms   258, 552, 558, 587

beds   44, 395, 449, 476, 494, 571

bed's   599

beeping   245, 246, 395, 396, 464, 552, 555

beeps   474

bees   467, 470

Beetee   315, 316, 317, 328, 331, 338, 339, 341, 343, 345, 348, 349, 363, 364, 366, 367, 368, 369, 370, 371, 372, 375, 377, 378, 379, 382, 383, 384, 385, 386, 387, 388, 389, 390, 391, 392, 393, 394, 396, 397, 406, 413, 425, 436, 437, 438, 439, 440, 441, 443, 457, 460, 463, 472, 473, 489, 493, 496, 497, 499, 505, 508, 509, 510, 524, 527, 535, 536, 556, 562, 576, 579, 590, 595, 596, 597, 602

Beetee's   339, 363, 364, 365, 367, 368, 372, 382, 384, 385, 386, 388, 389, 391,

392, 394, 396, 413, 414, 425, 458, 472, 475, 493, 518, 566, 575, 592

beetles 386

beets 464

before/after 465

befriending 121

befuddled 102

begged 2, 419

begging 138, 153, 179, 239, 289, 489, 526, 604

beginners 525, 531

beginner's 480

begins 10, 15, 20, 23, 32, 37, 51, 52, 65, 78, 84, 86, 92, 94, 96, 103, 107, 109, 116, 118, 126, 129, 132, 133, 136, 137, 145, 171, 174, 180, 188, 194, 196, 199, 206, 217, 224, 233, 235, 236, 249, 256, 257, 258, 259, 261, 263, 269, 275, 281, 286, 292, 296, 299, 308, 313, 314, 318, 333, 342, 350, 351, 354, 355, 356, 357, 359, 360, 361, 362, 365, 366, 367, 376, 378, 386, 388, 395, 400, 402, 409, 411, 414, 422, 426, 427, 444, 449, 450, 452, 454, 457, 464, 468, 472, 473, 474, 476, 485, 486, 491, 495, 502, 505, 521, 535, 537, 545, 552, 559, 560, 568, 570, 589, 590, 598, 606

begs 237, 282

beheaded 378

bejeweled 304

belches 593

believable 236

believably 157

believed 129, 212, 339, 530, 572, 573, 591

believes 165, 283, 474, 502, 504, 602

bellies 244, 519, 564

belligerently 269

bells 366

belonged 170, 216, 431

belongs 64, 85, 311, 395, 397, 452, 501

belts 308, 338

belt's 356, 364

bending 130, 181, 586

bends 155

benefits 474, 601

berries 5, 7, 88, 108, 111, 112, 114, 120, 121, 139, 146, 168, 169, 170, 172, 182, 183, 189, 190, 192, 195, 197, 208, 209, 233, 236, 239, 250, 260, 275, 302, 323, 398, 433, 441, 450, 522

berry container of 321

bestsellers 609

bestselling 609

betrayal 61

betrayal depth of 327

betrayal sense of 247

betrayals 491

betrayed   400, 412, 464
Betraying   541
bets   10, 129, 172, 297
betting   13, 31, 56, 62, 79, 81, 88, 89, 106, 120, 269, 334, 424
beverages   414
bewildered   494, 506
bids   193, 297
bigger   51, 59, 60, 97, 106, 301, 302, 372, 421
biggest   83, 84, 218, 283, 309, 355, 365, 533
billowing   547
billows   234, 514
bindings   593
bins   17, 114, 117, 523
birdcall   45, 467
birds   24, 34, 44, 45, 77, 87, 88, 103, 111, 115, 126, 128, 129, 149, 159, 160, 173, 229, 246, 247, 295, 302, 318, 343, 346, 375, 376, 377, 453, 466, 467, 468, 505, 506, 512, 556, 567, 585
bird's   395
Birds   98
birdsong   86, 126
birthdays   52, 161
birthrate   416
biscuits   53
bites   127, 154, 484, 498, 501
bits   3, 30, 34, 47, 65, 117, 118, 119, 135, 226, 231, 260, 284, 328, 394, 413, 418, 509, 546, 554, 566, 576, 607
bitterest   15
bitterly   148, 330, 372
bitterness   336, 442, 570
black   drone of   448
black   splatter of   550
blackberries   5, 29, 108
blacked   566
blackened   18, 94, 95, 196, 344, 405, 511
blackens   510
blackouts   67
blacks   552
blades   346
blaming   445, 483, 528
blanketed   403
blankets   15, 153, 291, 325, 480, 511
blanks   158, 545
blares   99
blasts   93
blatantly   267

blazes   42
blazing   362, 581
bleached   578
bled   81, 115, 195, 202, 310
blinded   495
blinds   528, 567
Blindsided   524
blinks   106, 281, 310, 408, 515
blissfully   95
blisters   95, 99, 103, 352
blocks   27, 231, 253, 332, 335, 375, 448, 453, 512, 551, 552, 562, 567, 568, 573, 576, 578, 580
blonde   7, 67, 176
blood   flow of   179, 302
blood   gush of   177
blood   scent of   357, 492
blood   smell of   237, 391
blood|I   208
blood|it   smell of   213
bloodbath   79, 81, 129, 192, 300, 336, 346
blooddappled   359
bloodied   548
bloodlust   446
bloodred   31, 88, 320
bloodstains   133
blooms   453, 514, 589
blossomed   202
blossoms   28, 126, 232, 339, 394, 457, 467, 564
blossoms   smell of   215
blots   487, 552
blotting   222
blows   166, 348, 453, 533, 546
blue   sheet of   170
blueberries   88
blueprints   508
bluntly   541
blurs   390
blurts   45, 441
blushes   70
blushing   73
boards   189
boats   306, 335
bobbing   190, 219, 338
bodied   404
bodies   36, 76, 81, 114, 125, 126, 131, 134, 240, 258, 267, 293, 311, 339, 353, 354, 356,

359, 360, 370, 383, 428, 431, 437, 447, 466, 489, 511, 516, 526, 527, 551, 556, 559, 565, 580, 582, 584

bodies   crush of   584

bodies   tumble of   547

bodyguards   442, 451, 459, 466

body's   189, 371, 506, 600

Boggs   416, 441, 442, 443, 444, 445, 447, 448, 449, 450, 451, 452, 455, 456, 457, 459, 461, 465, 471, 474, 475, 484, 485, 486, 488, 494, 495, 504, 508, 510, 512, 513, 524, 525, 533, 535, 538, 539, 540, 541, 542, 545, 546, 547, 548, 549, 550, 552, 554, 555, 560, 571, 572, 592, 606

Boggs's   416, 537, 539, 546, 550, 561, 562, 592

Boggs's   stump of   546

boldest   13

bolted   374, 577

bolt's   393

bombardment   395

bombed   272, 394, 416, 447, 454, 457, 509, 591

bombers   404, 451, 453

bombing   274, 414, 442, 447, 451, 452, 454, 456, 459, 461, 470, 472, 474, 479, 484, 485, 486, 487, 489, 490, 508, 590

bombings   412, 448, 484, 510, 538

bombs   45, 272, 396, 404, 451, 452, 453, 454, 458, 461, 479, 481, 482, 499, 544, 591, 593

bonding   293, 408

bones   5, 51, 105, 158, 172, 205, 279, 331, 341, 438, 478, 507, 600, 605, 606

Bong   350

bongs   365, 366

bonier   147

Bonnie   269, 270, 271, 272, 273, 274, 275, 279, 280, 282, 285, 318, 324, 397, 398, 409

Bonnie's   271, 273, 275, 277

booing   286

books   232, 446, 530

book's   281

booms   78, 130, 181, 190

boots   scuffle of   473

bordered   563

bordering   573

borders   385

bored   22, 28, 66, 92, 172, 278

borrowed   520

botched   80

bothered   12, 23, 38, 40, 57, 114, 266, 286, 454, 480, 534, 598

bothering   4, 217, 309, 560

bothers   314, 325, 388

bottles   134, 171, 173, 203, 256, 292, 471, 593, 603
boughs   345, 536
boulders   22, 134, 167
bounced   181
bounces   12, 67, 111, 386
bounding   533, 572
bounties   574
bouquets   229
bow| 102
bowels   558
bows   22, 49, 60, 190, 318, 337, 404, 422, 452, 499, 562, 581, 603
bow's   439
Bows   55
boxes   555, 576
boy| 423
boys   10, 12, 14, 46, 51, 70, 72, 85, 187, 201, 202, 223, 244, 502
boy's   13, 45, 119, 128, 129, 138, 288, 473, 486
Boys   20
braced   86, 403
bracelets   529
bragging   31
braids   34, 159, 333
brains   142, 177, 208, 246, 320, 505, 507, 508, 563, 574
brakes   462
branches   16, 27, 44, 83, 85, 87, 91, 92, 97, 98, 99, 101, 114, 164, 170, 219, 227,
246, 276, 284, 309, 339, 345, 346, 360, 373, 374, 376, 467, 605
branded   468
brashness   321
brats   17
bravely   299
braver   475, 608
breached   71, 556, 572
bread   loaves of   261, 490
breads   53, 70, 127, 239, 280
breaks   69, 85, 96, 101, 103, 115, 127, 135, 139, 166, 189, 190, 218, 220, 248, 249, 265,
298, 309, 329, 352, 410, 413, 426, 428, 467, 472, 501, 531, 544, 571
breasts   187, 223, 309, 317
breath   intake of   253
breathable   436
breathes   393
breaths   95, 205, 359, 477, 478
breathtakingly   102
breeders   416
breezes   349
brewed   5, 100, 414

brews 144
bricks 245, 266, 322, 402
briefly 112, 158, 239, 244, 311, 330, 336, 367, 392, 444, 506, 507, 536, 543, 561, 602
brightens 4, 141, 235, 348, 449, 500
brighter 67, 580, 588
brightest 326
brightly 24, 174, 204, 214, 223, 277, 310, 394, 425, 514, 529
brilliantly 40
brimming 465
bringing 106, 165, 219, 252, 274, 341, 427, 434, 546, 552
bringing effort of 342
brings 4, 12, 13, 26, 35, 70, 89, 125, 140, 152, 156, 172, 190, 204, 219, 220, 230, 237, 243, 315, 344, 346, 350, 377, 378, 381, 405, 447, 461, 477, 556, 564, 565, 588, 606, 608
Bristel 256, 257
bristled 47
broadcasts 425, 486
Broadway 609
Broiling 308
broken streets of 545
brothers 5, 15, 60, 200, 405, 595
brother's 327
brownouts 482
brows 183, 216, 217, 427, 439, 596
Brrr 206
bruised 27, 134, 279, 426, 517, 518, 525, 599
bruises 86, 105, 277, 434, 456, 494, 498, 499, 506, 560
bruising 495, 519
brush rustle of 168
brushed 16, 37, 239, 481
brushes 30, 140, 234, 560
brushing 214, 243, 246, 448, 481, 506, 511
brusquely 289, 445, 509
brutally 141
brute's 477
Brutus 296, 297, 311, 313, 314, 319, 323, 327, 331, 337, 338, 340, 356, 370, 382, 383, 385, 390, 394, 396, 398, 446
Brutus's 372, 390
bubbles 104, 291, 362, 433, 560, 564, 565
bubbling 95, 285
bucketful 68
buckets 163, 200, 385
buckled 17
buckles 239
budgets 208
bugged 279

buildings 9, 25, 32, 39, 229, 245, 247, 272, 447, 503, 533, 539, 544, 547, 548, 551, 582, 583, 584

builds 229

buildup 388

bulbs 67

bullets 514, 545, 546, 565, 581, 587

bull's 55

bumped 11

bumping 426

bunches 204, 346, 471

bunching 389

bundled 149, 254, 276, 567, 576, 580

bundles 579

BUNKER PROTOCOL 476

bunks 475, 476, 480

buns 203, 271, 281, 282, 544

burgundy 47

buried 32, 59, 124, 152, 370, 480, 603

buries 287, 298, 302, 358, 558, 586, 587

burn smell of 586

burns 37, 95, 98, 105, 106, 122, 132, 135, 140, 184, 195, 270, 290, 352, 457, 458, 553, 564, 588

burn's 95

burrowing 227

bursting 5

bursts 27, 31, 49, 55, 101, 126, 216, 289, 300, 303, 325, 334, 394, 413, 508, 520, 547, 594, 597

burying 349, 510

bushes 3, 4, 5, 22, 88, 106, 110, 116, 120, 196, 204, 300, 469, 604

bushes tangle of 118

busies 602

businesses 6, 16

But|how 330

but|I 310, 497

But|it 479

but|what 394

butchering 143

butcher's 17, 268

buts 32

Buttercup's 418, 419, 478, 480, 482, 484, 486

buttered temptation of 600

butters 57

buying 256, 271

buys 48, 135, 140, 203, 568

buzzards 9

buzzed 533

buzzing 44, 283, 429, 472, 510, 579

by|what 582

byes 40, 73, 244, 291, 294, 332

cabinets 471

cables 511, 548, 552

cadences 185

Caesar 67, 68, 69, 70, 71, 194, 195, 237, 286, 300, 326, 329, 330, 331, 412, 413, 414, 415, 450, 462

Caesar Flickerman 67, 160, 190, 191, 193, 194, 237, 238, 272, 285, 300, 327, 412, 461, 550

Caesar's 67, 68, 69, 328, 329, 331, 414

cages 295

caging 509

caked 134, 183, 258, 360

cakes 47, 52, 122, 133, 218, 242, 243, 267, 295, 419

called 3, 4, 5, 10, 11, 16, 23, 24, 25, 39, 45, 65, 69, 76, 212, 222, 226, 245, 259, 265, 270, 296, 297, 299, 306, 318, 320, 332, 345, 415, 434, 445, 456, 460, 467, 468, 519, 532, 533, 539, 544, 545, 555, 559, 585, 601

callously 177

calls 102, 124, 143, 166, 204, 245, 256, 296, 299, 312, 358, 362, 368, 383, 391, 432, 440, 449, 457, 466, 473, 490, 500, 522, 546, 552, 597

calmed 408, 468

calming 297, 489, 505

calmly 232, 258, 357, 541

calms 29, 47, 153, 184, 264

calories 122, 420

cameramen 447, 450, 456, 546

cameras 19, 22, 23, 32, 66, 67, 69, 70, 73, 87, 95, 119, 126, 131, 161, 164, 182, 186, 191, 194, 196, 197, 198, 202, 204, 205, 206, 207, 210, 214, 220, 233, 234, 235, 272, 276, 286, 291, 294, 298, 380, 440, 442, 447, 454, 455, 469, 492, 514, 516, 522, 534, 535, 548, 550, 552, 554, 558, 559, 562, 574, 578, 592, 594

camouflaged 166, 393

camouflaging 88, 91

campfires 113

campsite 346

canceled 148, 324, 332, 480

candies 277

candles 479

cannons 81, 102, 393

cans 211, 557

canvases 218

Cap Pryor 609

capabilities 397

capes 37, 38, 39, 47

Capitol| 394

Capitol's   8, 11, 24, 32, 35, 86, 98, 100, 188, 190, 196, 199, 219, 221, 248, 255, 261, 282, 295, 310, 320, 322, 324, 332, 335, 395, 398, 402, 410, 416, 423, 438, 441, 444, 445, 446, 466, 474, 486, 489, 490, 495, 496, 503, 510, 513, 520, 528, 538, 541, 572, 576, 584, 591, 595, 600

captors   544

capture   event of   539

captured   32, 76, 421, 423, 446, 467, 573, 583, 596, 599, 608

Capturing   592

carcasses   358

cared   190, 195, 211, 404, 413, 503

careens   363

Career Tributes   51, 53, 58, 68, 79, 82, 83, 85

Career pools of   296

Careers   51, 83, 85, 86, 87, 88, 93, 96, 97, 98, 99, 100, 101, 103, 105, 110, 111, 112, 114, 115, 116, 117, 118, 119, 120, 121, 122, 123, 126, 128, 129, 130, 131, 132, 173, 192, 230, 292, 301, 313, 337, 345, 348, 355, 362, 368, 372, 383, 384, 388, 390, 391, 543

carefully   2, 3, 5, 10, 17, 27, 34, 37, 39, 46, 57, 82, 83, 104, 116, 117, 142, 151, 174, 183, 188, 200, 263, 273, 280, 281, 320, 326, 329, 350, 376, 392, 403, 414, 424, 438, 478, 483, 514, 596, 597

carefully   aisles of   589

carelessly   143, 151, 254, 379, 533

carelessness   212

cares   14, 56, 72, 75, 84, 94, 105, 224, 305, 362, 478, 494, 553, 601

caresses   140

caring   13, 128, 214, 394

carpeted   599

carpets   19, 588

carried   17, 45, 174, 256, 259, 352, 362, 455, 493, 515, 565, 584, 599

carries   3, 13, 107, 269, 280, 282, 358, 359, 363, 548, 598, 601

carrying   76, 82, 94, 142, 184, 192, 270, 302, 375, 385, 392, 537, 607

cars   32, 44, 226, 472, 575

carted   506

carts   53, 317, 447, 486, 605

cart's   605

carved   113, 208, 232, 476

Cashmeres   492

Cashmere's   370

Castor's   558

casts   304

casually   240, 281, 283, 305, 315, 340, 357

casualties   81, 138, 510, 538, 576

Cat Adoration   411

catacombs   76, 77

catatonic   238

catches   2, 79, 92, 100, 116, 119, 139, 150, 158, 220, 234, 245, 247, 283, 294, 312, 313, 317, 334, 336, 352, 375, 378, 397, 400, 408, 412, 428, 436, 447, 454, 461, 470, 478, 523, 530, 583, 585, 591, 604, 608

Catching Fire   1, 198, 609

Catching Fire Dedication Table   610

caters   5

Cato   97, 103, 105, 114, 115, 119, 120, 128, 131, 132, 133, 134, 139, 141, 145, 147, 151, 152, 153, 154, 155, 156, 162, 163, 164, 166, 167, 168, 170, 171, 172, 173, 174, 175, 176, 177, 178, 179, 180, 181, 192, 237, 446, 467, 496, 512

Cato   threat of   171

Cato|and   515

Cato's   118, 119, 128, 135, 136, 152, 153, 166, 167, 169, 170, 177, 178, 180, 181, 192, 226, 320, 503, 512

Cato's   sound of   153

cats   2, 28, 501

cat's   223, 353, 479, 573

caused   105, 142, 222, 245, 272, 303, 461, 464, 492

causes   118, 134, 162, 165, 222, 258, 328, 352, 399, 422, 481, 520

causing   118, 216, 362, 386, 398, 453, 509, 578

caustically   497

cautiously   35, 100, 127, 529

cavelike   137

caves   504

caving   435

ceased   245, 489, 526

ceases   366

Cecelia   296, 317, 348

ceilings   395

celebrating   131, 323

celebrations   185, 207, 211, 217

celebrities   303

celebrity   price of   596

cells   529, 586, 599

centered   260, 431

centers   24, 272, 544

centralized   446

centuries   287, 409, 503, 586

ceremonies   30, 36, 37, 40, 43, 57, 69, 196, 211, 236, 296, 304, 305, 307, 311

ceremony's   230

chafes   495

Chaff's   382

chairs   10, 19, 21, 208, 227, 239, 552

chalk   boxes of   471

challenged   53, 195, 483

challenges   595

champions 298
chances 12, 148, 435, 554, 578
changed 49, 195, 229, 234, 251, 273, 279, 280, 311, 434, 437, 496, 527, 569, 597, 603
changes 38, 500, 546
changing 35, 308, 447, 559, 564
chanting 450
chaperoned 40
chaperones 71
chapped 252, 259
charges 491, 546
charging 267, 533
chariots 37, 38, 39, 305, 311, 485
chariots procession of 307
Charles Pryor 198, 609
Charlie 401, 609
charmingly 209
charms 528
charred 87, 95, 270, 274, 315, 328, 402, 466
chased 53, 467, 490
chases 261
chattered 311
chattering 111, 119, 179, 307
chatters 284
chatting 309, 500
cheaper 558
checking 17, 32, 85, 264, 376, 402, 408, 437, 455, 478, 546, 564
checks 169, 279, 421, 425, 426, 437, 463, 476, 551
cheekbones 304, 581
cheeks 2, 16, 55, 62, 71, 72, 125, 184, 202, 219, 239, 250, 340, 342, 348, 349, 375, 410, 415, 423, 469, 477, 606
cheered 58
cheerfully 97, 499
cheering 58, 148, 193, 199, 236, 286, 473
cheers 38, 69, 190, 229, 521, 598
cheese.| 169
cheeses 21, 239
chemicals 352
chemicals mixture of 558
cherries 295
chestnuts 248, 249, 250
chests 191, 232
chewed 107, 140
chewed handful of 136
chews 470

Chickens 35
children's 165, 591, 601
child's 24, 106, 123, 358, 542
chilled 16, 30, 139, 202, 209, 259
chimes 44, 45, 278, 325
chiming 569
chimneys 204
chinks 345, 537
chinning 320
chipped 203
chips 283
chives 141
choices 48, 234, 260, 426, 508, 510
choked 14, 194, 441, 601
chokes 71, 210, 260
chooses 14, 346
choosier 7
choosing 250, 286, 348
chopped 577, 588
Christopher Santos 609
chronically 271
chucking 133, 346
chuckles 496
chuckling 30, 69
chugging 560
chunks 7, 17, 35, 61, 304, 478, 546, 565
cinders 511
Cinna 34, 35, 36, 37, 38, 39, 41, 43, 44, 46, 47, 48, 54, 57, 59, 62, 64, 65, 66, 68, 69, 70, 71, 72, 73, 76, 77, 78, 185, 186, 187, 188, 189, 190, 191, 193, 196, 199, 206, 215, 217, 218, 219, 220, 223, 224, 227, 228, 232, 234, 235, 236, 243, 245, 268, 283, 284, 286, 303, 304, 305, 307, 308, 309, 311, 312, 322, 323, 325, 326, 327, 328, 329, 333, 334, 335, 343, 349, 407, 418, 424, 425, 427, 431, 433, 443, 446, 451, 456, 481, 486, 517, 520, 570, 586, 592, 606
Cinna   image of 335
Cinna| I'm 66
cinnamon   scent of 516
Cinna's 34, 36, 37, 38, 43, 63, 73, 78, 94, 188, 190, 219, 247, 248, 251, 252, 268, 304, 331, 334, 335, 424, 426, 434, 451, 478, 520, 521, 585, 599
Cinna's Mockingjay 595
Circenses 519
circled 47
circles 31, 45, 78, 103, 213, 236, 362, 398, 433, 465, 560, 606
Circle's 584
circling 345, 362, 363, 374, 402
circumstances 96, 99, 132, 291, 294, 313, 379, 403, 423, 442, 459, 467, 475, 566, 595
circumstances|how 234

circuses 519

cities 545

citizens 10, 39, 65, 209, 306, 410, 416, 428, 446, 474, 479, 491, 504, 509, 568, 572, 577, 581

City Circle 37, 39, 67, 70, 308, 311, 573, 584, 587, 592, 598, 599

City Circle's 577

city's 37

civilians 576

civilizing 41

claimed 67, 77, 191

claiming 92, 325, 383, 476

claims 140

clamped 429, 511, 567, 599

clamps 182, 339

clanks 228

clapping 220, 521

claps 13

clarifies 413

clasps 237

classically 296

classier 31

Claudius 130, 145, 457

Claudius Templesmith 78, 88, 145, 147, 149, 182, 350, 458

Claudius Templesmith's 130, 181

Claudius voice of 334

claustrophobic 10, 200, 495

clawed 440, 565

clawing 177, 599

claws 176, 261, 357, 565, 586

cleaned 64, 81, 87, 134, 567

cleaners smell of 322

cleans 64, 361, 579

cleared 59, 77, 102, 194, 253, 256, 264, 265, 266, 283, 408, 460, 565

clearer 138, 354

clears 257, 321, 456

clenched 12, 178, 199, 447

clenches 526

clenching 78, 103, 376, 511

cleverness 40, 114

clicked 150

clicking 379, 386, 389, 391, 400

clicks 213, 302, 444, 507, 558

clicks sound of 386

clients 28

climbed 2, 14, 132, 168, 179, 197, 516

climbing		28, 89, 96, 103, 175, 452, 485
climbs	15, 19, 38, 54, 237, 527	
clinches		586
clinging		18, 22, 299, 346, 463, 494
clings	583, 586	
clinking		603
clipboards		501, 522, 562
clips	228, 282, 461, 473	
cloaks	568, 579	
clocked		200
clogged		510
closely	5, 95, 135, 184, 229, 449, 465, 503, 506	
closeness		305, 324
closes	7, 20, 64, 180, 183, 185, 536, 543	
closest	2, 171, 268, 336, 371, 580	
closets	567	
clothed		177, 329
clothing's		104
cloths	141, 448	
clots	599	
clouds	18, 94, 149, 239, 240, 300, 355, 445, 446, 501, 564, 602	
Clove memories of		512
Clove|and		515
Clove|she		155
Clove's		150, 152, 155, 503
clubs	79	
clucking		311
clues	123	
clumps		604
clumsily		98, 392, 542
clunker		148
Clusters		114
clutched		18, 205, 371, 495
clutches		134, 364, 449, 485, 546, 607
clutching		60, 80, 290, 374, 463, 530, 576, 603
coached		61
coaching		61, 66, 197, 218, 324
coal color of		328
coal layer of		16
coals	87, 88, 106, 167, 170, 205, 304	
coats	188, 390, 567, 568, 579	
coaxes	291, 470, 485	
coaxing		138, 144, 170, 498, 586
cobblestones		265
cockily		534

cocks	467	
cocooned	2	
coerced	509	
coffee's	485	
coils	227, 255	
Coin I'd	432	
Coin|	444	
coins	203, 257, 258	
Coin's	406, 415, 416, 424, 428, 436, 441, 478, 479, 520, 577, 587, 589, 590	
coldhearted	510	
coldly	524	
coldness	263	
collaborating	415	
collapse	verge of	570
collapsed	110, 402, 454, 551	
collapses	255, 302, 353, 362, 490, 553, 598	
collapsing	118, 328, 458, 472	
colleagues	596	
collecting	46, 169, 203, 227, 476	
collects	346, 377, 486, 578	
collides	178	
color|it's	543	
colors	32, 88, 126, 156, 176, 256, 304, 321, 398, 533, 588, 589	
columns	228	
combat	middle of	441
combed	203	
combing	36, 84, 291	
comes	12, 23, 24, 25, 44, 54, 58, 64, 66, 72, 75, 76, 96, 99, 105, 107, 108, 118, 124, 149, 150, 160, 167, 168, 169, 174, 187, 192, 193, 203, 205, 213, 216, 218, 222, 227, 228, 234, 251, 255, 258, 262, 263, 278, 279, 281, 285, 292, 297, 302, 304, 306, 307, 324, 327, 328, 331, 335, 339, 340, 341, 344, 349, 352, 354, 355, 362, 369, 378, 382, 399, 412, 420, 424, 426, 434, 436, 438, 439, 443, 444, 447, 451, 458, 478, 492, 495, 496, 504, 508, 513, 515, 517, 526, 527, 530, 535, 549, 550, 556, 562, 566, 571, 574, 578, 582, 583, 587, 588, 593, 595, 596, 603, 604, 606	
comfortably	412	
comforted	127, 164, 482, 570	
comforting	24, 111, 124, 140, 185, 202, 303, 427	
comforts	29, 372	
comically	26	
coming	shock of	480
Command	doorway of	411
Commander Paylor	447	
commanders	510, 539	
commander's	539	
commands	127, 336, 439, 556, 562, 581	

commentators   25, 88, 600

comments   48, 85, 214, 226, 228, 229, 244, 296, 297, 318, 324, 428, 440, 442, 594

committed   42, 237, 259

committing   262

commotion   sounds of   216

Communication Center   272

communications   396, 601

communicator   429, 547

communicators   463, 549

communicuff   411, 416, 420, 464

communities   227

companions   30, 114, 119, 176, 351, 363, 370, 567, 570

compared   8, 12, 89, 101, 201, 426, 435

comparing   61, 70, 156, 212

comparisons   564

compartments   404, 484

compartments beehive of   524

compatibility   575

competing   59, 82, 224, 588

competition|best   161

competitors   11, 80, 126, 130, 300, 303, 305, 313

complaining   498, 537

complains   264

complaints   283, 455

completed   164, 388, 486

completely   25, 34, 39, 66, 67, 76, 77, 80, 102, 115, 131, 133, 146, 161, 166, 171, 179, 180, 189, 205, 212, 223, 249, 278, 292, 294, 299, 324, 328, 334, 361, 373, 374, 385, 386, 402, 415, 446, 449, 459, 464, 482, 491, 519, 549, 571, 580, 588, 592, 607

completes   331

complimenting   68

compliments   66

composes   62, 552

computerized   411

computers   436, 493

comrades   440, 512

concealed   3, 45, 85, 87, 93, 94, 115, 273, 283, 315, 362, 368, 374, 555

concealing   188, 320, 349, 352, 391, 448

conceals   446, 584

conceivably   25

conceived   93

concentrates   281

concerns   3, 115, 275, 385, 429, 495, 503, 521

concocted   202, 204

concoctions   223, 239, 414

condemned   395

condemning	130, 415
condemns	278
condenses	80
Condensing	191
conditions	209, 245, 415, 422, 445, 450, 480, 558, 569, 572, 580
conducted	19, 40
conducts	521
confessed	225, 254
confidentially	69, 518
confines	366, 379
confining	193, 313
confirming	392, 409, 467
confirms	39, 57, 173, 337, 370, 427, 454, 567
confiscated	418
confiscating idea of	575
conflicted	18, 554
conflicting	84, 153, 207, 565
confrontation	147
confrontational	215
confronted	447
confronting	94
confused	7, 11, 28, 73, 79, 87, 103, 137, 168, 177, 197, 327, 380, 392, 417, 482, 501, 576
confusing	130, 194, 498
congealed	367
congestion	563
congratulates	533, 555
congratulating	58, 130
congratulations	37, 85, 194, 512
Congress Cataloging	609
Connecticut	609
connecting	530
connects	102, 510, 557, 568
conquers	511
consented	432
considerably	171, 235, 356, 518, 558
considerations	404
considers	31, 162, 435, 477, 508, 525
consistently	7, 81
consisting	11
consists	447, 476
consoles	440
conspicuously	247
conspiratorial	238
conspiratorially	97

constantly	43, 60, 193, 240, 531, 571
constants	35
constructed	66, 229
constructions	265
construed	432
consults	459
consumed	165, 240, 253, 324, 495, 607
consumes	179, 335, 481
consuming	215, 571
contacted	47
contained	540
containers	78, 116, 119, 140, 174
containing	153, 184, 295, 567
contains	14, 117, 418, 440, 534
contemplating	46
contender	75, 531
contents	1, 80, 136, 153, 198, 278, 321, 401, 476, 478, 604, 610
contestants	22, 23, 181, 206
continued	89, 245, 353
continues	70, 112, 116, 158, 273, 287, 351, 377, 413, 432, 475, 502, 504, 508, 512, 524, 526, 534, 535, 553, 582, 585, 604
continuing	88, 301, 353, 513
continuously	187, 501
contortions	353
contorts	473, 579
contracting	42
contracts	371, 428
contributed	100, 500
contributes	107
contributing	216, 607
controlled	187, 246, 534, 556
controlling	420
controls	93
converging	335, 475
conversations	24, 293, 310
conveyed	599
conveys	529
convinced	37, 60, 130, 208, 222, 252, 307, 338, 366, 373, 382, 384, 402, 504
convinces	549
convincingly	165, 309, 398
convulses	94
convulsing	437
cooked	15, 35, 92, 170, 347, 384, 434
cooked|	347
cookie bits of	214

cookies		21, 27, 33, 46, 209, 210, 218, 226, 555, 575, 606
cookies	packet of	27
cooks	35, 87, 431, 603	
cooled	18, 349, 485	
cooling		83, 100, 137
coolly	7, 387	
cools	139	
cooperating		402
coordinates		556, 559
copying		22
coring	248	
corners		235, 296, 533, 590
Cornucopia's		369
corpses		448, 582
corrected		26
corrects		213, 278, 535, 588
corresponding		369
corresponds		559
corridors		429
corrupted		466, 504
cosmetically		314
costs	413	
costumed		485, 514
costumes		36, 40, 42, 43, 75, 94, 188, 218, 286, 308, 311, 312
cots	448	
couches		35, 227
cougars		3
coughed		81
coughing		92, 135, 370, 548, 590, 598
coughs		21, 41, 80, 96, 176, 598
could|	420	
could've		159, 293, 320, 330, 418, 438, 443, 444, 506, 567
counted		7, 40, 212, 246, 350
countered		435
countering		510
counterparts		493
counters		313
counterstrike		474
countertop		255
counting		121, 182, 247, 259, 571
counts	194, 312, 379, 387	
couples		43, 241
cousins		204, 208, 213, 408, 422
cousin's		518
Cover Page		1

covering precaution of 109
covers 3, 36, 46, 59, 74, 168, 219, 221, 237, 261, 268, 304, 396, 434, 441, 521, 529, 551
cover's 558
Covers 488, 579
cowed 426
cows 239, 308, 311
cozier 509
crabmeat 283
crackers 82, 91, 108, 116, 579
crackles 440
cracks 82, 165, 226, 250, 266, 328, 443, 478, 483, 548, 583
cradled 111, 590
cradles 498
crafted 3, 7
cramps 176
cranked 331
crashes 71, 94, 101, 103, 374, 453, 461
craters 485
crates 114, 117, 447
crawled 18, 365
crawling 2, 3, 297, 307, 449, 471, 538, 564
crawls 291, 354
Cray 203, 251, 253, 256, 257, 258, 280, 306, 491
Cray's 256
Crazy Cat 482, 484
creams 223
creased 183, 320
creases 253, 260
created 104, 219, 246, 347, 482, 502, 534, 595
creating 24, 185, 246, 286, 315, 369, 547
creators 328
creatures 82, 98, 171, 176, 239, 241, 354, 357, 384, 456, 562
creature's 347
credited 129
creepers 352, 373
creepiest 469
creeping 116, 265, 346, 493
Cressida 447, 450, 453, 454, 456, 458, 459, 460, 461, 463, 465, 466, 469, 470, 472, 484, 486, 487, 490, 513, 531, 538, 546, 548, 549, 550, 552, 561, 562, 565, 566, 567, 568, 569, 570, 571, 572, 573, 578, 579, 580, 583, 587, 605
Cressida's 455, 459, 487, 490, 566
crested 374, 548
crests 362
crewmate 605
crewmates 256

crews	9, 67, 199, 211, 281, 537
crew's	485, 490
cried	2, 16, 291, 441
cries	29, 71, 85, 101, 134, 178, 269, 407, 511
crimes	237, 280, 396, 489, 573, 595
criminals	228, 423, 427
crippled	25, 68
crises	474
crisscrossed	483
critically	52
croaking	354
croaks	396, 449
croons	479
cropped	34, 444
crops	108, 227
crosses	12, 14, 37, 74, 80, 121, 168, 205, 327, 367, 469, 480, 501, 518, 570, 601
crossing	task of 542
crouched	275, 403, 606
crouches	247, 359, 368, 512
Crouching	92
crowds	43, 148, 199, 236, 237, 248, 272, 485
crowd's	25, 38, 192, 253
cruelties	320
crumbling	228, 256
crumbs	213
crumpling	238
crunched	599
crunching	305
crunchy	164, 430
crushed	321, 323, 438, 600, 601
crusts	17
cubes	309, 386, 456, 485
cuffed	552, 566
culled	520
culminating	286
cupboards	555
cups	100, 209, 253, 271, 435, 484, 534
curiously	174, 316
curled	2, 15, 56, 125, 191, 212, 216, 415, 419, 471
curlicues	581
curls	11, 216, 327, 389, 414, 426, 429, 449, 500, 578, 607
currently	397, 430, 445, 448
currents	336
cursing	158
curtains	30, 261, 266, 588

curved	78, 124, 151, 177, 223, 232, 345, 397
curves	187, 348
cushioned	409, 588
cushions	557
customers	3, 142, 569
cuts	98, 101, 105, 240, 250, 255, 289, 343, 355, 374, 422, 478, 487, 494, 606
cylinders	443
dabbing	105, 296
dabbles	359
dabs	166, 213, 465, 545, 590
daggers	327
daisies	125, 608
Dalton	405, 440, 442, 449, 521
damaged	96, 142, 149, 261, 319, 355, 356, 360, 364, 380, 391, 430, 433, 454, 462, 484, 497, 587, 588, 599
dampening	139
dances	240
dancing	75, 241, 245, 521, 523, 607
dandelions	27
danger emergence of	150
dangerously	105, 127, 276, 367
dangers	93, 237, 337, 362, 422
dangles	320, 336, 460
dangling	52, 95, 122, 152, 300, 314
dared	109, 494
Darius	203, 251, 256, 310, 311, 312, 317, 349, 507, 545, 560, 562
Darius's	255, 310, 312, 335
Dark Days	10, 273, 282, 286, 331, 409, 410, 416, 445, 503, 519, 534, 591
dark sticks of	417
darkened	186, 243
darkens	12, 417, 546
darker	39
darkly	317
darts	150, 301, 436, 539
dates	471
David Levithan	608
dawn crack of	4
dawning	100
dawns	170, 483, 533, 535
day light of	570
daydreaming	122
daydreams	368
daylight's	324
day's	29, 30, 82, 84, 113, 228, 275, 464, 579
dazed	431, 584

dazzled 78
dazzling 38, 190, 236, 350, 386, 394, 490, 521, 586
deactivated 559, 573
deactivating 576
dead| 402, 599
deadened 590
deadens 121
deadliest 36, 51
deadliness 149
dead's 81
deafened 119
deafness 121
deals 41, 49, 338
death cause of 16
deaths 22, 77, 81, 92, 100, 109, 129, 156, 163, 177, 191, 492, 596, 597, 607
death's 9, 233, 600
debilitating 352
debts 127, 446
decades 12, 232, 474
decapitated 564, 572
deceived 414
deceleration 370
decently 42, 503
deceptions 398
deceptively 304
decidedly 386
decides 113, 116, 247, 250, 319, 598
deciding 45, 151, 262, 330, 342, 390, 522
decimated 416, 538
decisions 383, 520, 574
decked 127
decks 326
declares 527
declaring 490
declining 145, 492
decompiled 609
decomposing 361, 466
decorated 242, 486, 529, 548, 567
decorating 36, 133
decorations 520
decrees 207
deducted 422
deeds 509
deemed 282, 414, 587
deems 525

deepening 38
deeper 28, 46, 82, 100, 352, 391, 449, 549, 551, 603
deepest 589
defeated 10, 16, 513, 596
defender 517, 528
defending 413, 430, 544, 572
defense| 437
defenseless 121, 125, 358, 444, 491, 562
defenses 271, 331, 538, 572, 591
defensively 327, 333, 415
defiantly 57, 514
defied 231
defiled 267
defined 460
definitions 432
deflated 122
deflating 427
deflecting 346
deflects 292
deftly 42, 361
defuse 250
defusing 231
defying 90, 191, 213, 324, 406
degrees 139, 249, 355, 397
dehydrated 105
dehydrating 88
dehydration 82, 173, 340
dehydration days of 333
dehydration threat of 346
delayed 571
delaying 332, 334
deliberately 340
delicacies 11, 43, 64, 223, 239
Delicately 589
delineated 476
delivered 18, 89, 211, 295, 504
delivers 400, 417
Delly 42, 500, 501, 502, 528, 529, 530, 532, 586
Delly Cartwright 42, 43, 500
Delly's 500, 502
deluded 89
deluding 455, 458
deluged 47
delusional 552
delusions 274, 428

demanded	217
demands	152, 201, 224, 250, 331, 421, 458, 473, 504, 542, 545, 549
demeaning	372, 423
demolished	410, 465
demolishing	117
demonstrated	172, 309, 488
demonstrations	55
demoralized	555
demotion	416
denied	351, 419
denies	540
dense patches of	339
departments	41
depended	45
depending	199, 544
depends	252, 336, 490, 508
depicting	311
depiction	460
depleted	271
depleting	576
deposited	243, 267, 552, 599
deprecating	63
depresses	532
depressing	164
depths	200, 362
derailed	275, 472, 571
descending	115, 222, 225, 253, 547
descends	193, 240, 425
describes	330
describing	250, 440, 461
descriptions	281
deserting	538
deserves	278
designated	201, 224, 253, 429, 492
designates	316
designating	433
designs	64, 188, 218, 219, 232, 286, 499, 590
desperately	12, 35, 68, 74, 94, 145, 146, 153, 182, 189, 238, 306, 342, 374, 506
despises	207
Despite Haymitch's	52, 193
destinations	77, 582
destroyed	41, 95, 99, 110, 166, 273, 285, 304, 384, 481, 484, 525, 538, 544, 607
destroying	112, 115, 395, 531, 601
destroys	210, 403
destruction path of	105

destruction trail of 450
detaches 517
details 69, 160, 221, 265, 274, 411, 469, 520, 544, 559, 591, 606
detained 427
detected 486
detection danger of 492
detectors 437
deteriorated 29, 283, 462, 589
determinedly 567
determines 495
determining 433
detonates 451, 547
detonating 583, 584
devastated 450
developed 409, 453, 462, 534
deviance 433
devices 326, 338, 498, 589
devised 181, 287, 544
devising 85
devoting 423
devours 328, 481, 604
dials 183, 559, 560
diamonds 40, 283, 309
Dick Robinson 608
dictated 286
dictates 26
did| 6
did|even 6
died 22, 91, 95, 103, 111, 119, 124, 127, 138, 144, 152, 153, 158, 163, 172, 176, 211, 258, 260, 287, 340, 348, 349, 352, 378, 381, 391, 398, 409, 413, 441, 456, 468, 482, 483, 489, 504, 511, 561, 568, 572, 600, 601
dies 124, 175, 180, 182, 229, 302, 311, 339, 358, 369, 380, 440, 572
differed 271
differences 519, 593, 601
difficulties 422
digesting 87
digging 28, 91, 226, 238, 381, 390, 523, 546, 561, 604, 606
digs 12, 107, 261, 447
dilated 364, 566
dimensions 570
diminishes 121, 354
dimming 98, 255
dining 24, 30, 41, 47, 53, 54, 61, 62, 73, 187, 220, 222, 224, 226, 239, 310, 311, 312, 316, 319, 321, 411, 420, 434, 441, 464, 520, 528, 530
dinners 236

dinnertime	471, 603	
dipped	103, 239, 362, 551	
dipping	30, 47, 210, 213, 301, 518	
dips	119, 378	
directing	90, 301, 309, 447, 580	
directness	209	
directs	62, 76, 329, 466, 475, 553	
dirt clods of	604	
dirt traces of	134	
disappeared	17, 171, 197, 222, 438, 600	
disappearing	80, 83, 171, 180, 185, 210, 235, 242	
disappears	39, 76, 101, 128, 133, 134, 187, 189, 201, 237, 242, 338, 370, 498, 518, 569	
disappointing idea of	57	
disappointingly	456	
disapproving	216	
disarmed	302	
disarms	301	
disasters	10	
discarded	205, 587	
discarding	182	
discharged	498, 527	
disclosed	181	
disconnects	542	
discouraged	497, 503	
discouraging	115	
discovered	18, 87, 116, 246, 313, 382, 463, 559, 601	
discrepancies	426	
discussed	46	
discussing	4, 210, 379, 589, 597	
disembarks	447	
disengages	299	
disengaging	60	
disfigured	102, 431	
disgorged	511	
disgruntled	26	
disguised	133, 273	
disguises	52, 573	
Disgusted	434	
disgusts	555	
dishes	24, 47, 64, 122, 141, 234, 240, 295, 419, 464, 578, 603	
dishing	162	
disinformation	538	
disintegrates	102, 262	
disintegrating	226, 375	

disintegrators   471
disks   32
disliked   258, 408
dislikes   201
disliking   28
dislodges   301
dismantled   551
dismissed   18, 55, 57, 415
dismisses   65
dismissing   209
dismissively   387, 524
disobeyed   456, 540
disoriented   104, 392, 411, 472, 499, 581, 587
disorients   300
dispatched   279
dispensed   255
dispersed   81
displaced   492, 576, 577
displays   581
disregarded   459
disregarding   474
disrupted   234
dissecting   88
dissolves   174, 516
distances   357
distastefully   484
distorting   316
distractedly   320, 520
distracting   80, 97, 444
distractions   173, 240
distracts   77, 242, 368
distributed   493
District Eight   250, 251, 252, 269, 273, 454, 457
District Eleven   108, 156, 222, 227, 229
District Ten   528
District Thirteen   11, 270, 273, 423, 501
District Twelve   3, 34, 35, 36, 38, 49, 58, 63, 68, 70, 72, 76, 151, 155, 163, 170,
197, 233, 243, 279, 330, 336, 343, 380, 400, 515
District   citizens of   404
District   fence of   99
District   fences of   167
District   law of   433
district lives of   251
District   mines of   282
District   outskirts of   273

District	people of	13, 127, 189, 231, 262, 272
District	population of	294
District	rest of	241
District	ruins of	45
District	safety of	3
District	size of	227
District	streets of	142
District	tributes of	182, 230

district|making 14

district|they 152

districts 8, 10, 11, 13, 20, 23, 24, 32, 51, 53, 68, 70, 77, 86, 99, 108, 111, 196, 199, 208, 209, 213, 217, 228, 231, 233, 234, 237, 241, 246, 250, 260, 268, 272, 275, 283, 284, 285, 286, 288, 293, 296, 303, 324, 329, 330, 331, 351, 397, 406, 407, 409, 411, 417, 440, 444, 446, 448, 450, 455, 458, 462, 465, 472, 473, 490, 502, 503, 512, 515, 518, 519, 524, 541, 587, 590, 591, 592, 596, 597

district's 36, 218, 400, 403

Districts 85, 109, 213, 284, 293, 296, 313

distrustfully 569

distrusts 2

disturbingly 172

disturbs 99

dives 337, 356, 586

divides 383, 516

dividing 60, 156, 453, 489

diving 215, 458, 511, 546

divisions 532

dizziness 119, 370

dizzying 461

DNA 437

doctored 556

doctors 5, 183, 257, 344, 402, 407, 456, 494, 495, 496, 498, 518, 526, 586

doctors audience of 522

Document Outline 610

documenting 211

dodges 606

dodging 93, 192

doesn't 8, 13, 15, 19, 20, 21, 30, 31, 40, 41, 44, 46, 50, 58, 66, 68, 69, 73, 74, 75, 76, 85, 89, 94, 96, 99, 103, 104, 108, 109, 117, 118, 126, 132, 140, 145, 146, 147, 148, 154, 157, 158, 165, 168, 169, 170, 174, 178, 186, 197, 199, 203, 204, 206, 209, 220, 223, 226, 228, 229, 230, 232, 234, 235, 239, 242, 246, 249, 250, 251, 252, 255, 256, 257, 258, 264, 267, 268, 270, 274, 282, 283, 284, 290, 295, 301, 302, 305, 309, 314, 317, 325, 326, 328, 329, 333, 334, 339, 347, 348, 355, 364, 367, 371, 372, 373, 375, 380, 383, 385, 387, 396, 399, 404, 405, 406, 413, 415, 416, 418, 420, 421, 432, 434, 435, 438, 449, 451, 453, 456, 459, 461, 464, 465, 466, 472, 474, 481, 483, 493, 496, 498, 501, 506, 515, 517, 520, 522, 524, 526, 527, 528, 532, 535, 536, 539, 540, 541, 542, 545, 560, 561, 562, 569, 572, 582, 583, 584, 587, 588, 589, 592, 594,

595, 599, 605

doggedly   118, 338

dogging   53

dogs   3, 28, 96, 199, 469, 470, 508

dolphins   531

dominated   71

don't| 210

don't|find   462, 463

doomed   18, 213

Doorknobs   583

doors   6, 23, 28, 37, 39, 46, 51, 55, 71, 184, 186, 204, 216, 228, 231, 232, 240, 263, 295, 307, 308, 309, 321, 419, 425, 426, 444, 477, 478, 479, 512, 514, 527, 538, 557, 570, 577, 582, 583, 589, 598

door's   438

doorways   266, 475, 546, 581

doubled   176

doubted   165, 233, 323, 432

doubtfully   345, 361

doubts   130, 210, 380, 483, 509, 602

douses   205

dovetails   324

downgraded   475

downloaded   609

dozed   12, 85, 138, 164

Dr. Aurelius   587, 588, 601, 604

Dr. Aurelius's   606

Dr. Everdeen   136

drafts   608

dragged   118, 162, 263, 266, 267, 320, 362, 407, 552, 599

dragger   362

drags   52, 159, 199, 514, 526

drained   12, 30, 173, 571

draining   183

drainpipes   562

drains   137, 387

dramatically   304, 605

draped   306, 478, 552, 555

drapes   129, 329, 579, 594

Draping   586

drawbacks   422

drawings   27, 222, 227, 281, 501

draws   12, 95, 274, 378, 383, 467, 518, 588

dreaded   331

dreading   150, 198, 199, 347

dreamed   63, 239, 398, 500

dreamily	37
dreamless	18
dreamlike	240
dreams	2, 30, 47, 125, 237, 261, 333, 412, 457, 516, 531, 608
dredged	469
drenched	94
drenches	526
dress|there	160
dressed	32, 36, 37, 41, 42, 51, 52, 66, 68, 186, 219, 236, 239, 245, 269, 283, 284, 286, 299, 304, 307, 308, 339, 352, 425, 434, 445, 520, 526, 531, 589
dresses	9, 193, 254, 267, 279, 280, 282, 284, 286, 306, 326, 465, 520
dries	134, 201, 291
drifted	144, 259, 268
drifting	96, 261, 516, 556, 563
drifts	179, 264, 350, 360, 365, 561, 571
drilled	229, 349
drills	474, 531
drink clutches of	311
drinks	140, 203, 206, 607
drippings	164
drips	103, 107, 154, 156
drives	124, 129, 200, 224, 267, 306, 349
drizzled	239
drones	471
droning	245
drooling	306, 523, 577
droops	352
droplets	351, 352, 356, 359, 476
dropped	16, 18, 45, 57, 64, 70, 117, 171, 212, 214, 241, 249, 330, 337, 356, 400, 403, 486, 504, 506, 508, 516, 591, 592, 595
droughts	10
drowned	356, 405, 452, 477
drowning	124, 338, 466
drowns	38
drowsiness	96, 111
drugged	327, 441, 590, 601
drugging	154
drugs	140, 166, 260, 296, 402, 497, 526, 536
Drugs Peeta	441
drugs haze of	237
drumming	342, 548
drumsticks	255
drunkards	292
drunkenness	398
drunks	11

dryness 82
ducking 546
dulling 412
dullness 92
dulls 516
dully 399
dumbfounded 373
dummies 320, 536, 537
dummy's 52, 320
dumping 129, 558
dungeons 436, 444
dunking 368
dunks 58, 363, 368
duplicitous 225
dust coat of 232
dusted 511
duties 23, 40, 386, 429, 476, 498, 524
dwindling 176
dyed 34, 187, 237
dyes 67, 284, 321, 433
eagerly 33, 86, 197, 267, 405, 513, 584
eagerness 186, 218, 429, 446
earlier 15, 21, 46, 47, 82, 93, 156, 181, 191, 192, 225, 235, 253, 291, 392, 413, 453, 507, 528
earliest 569, 609
earmuffs 219
earned 541, 602
earnestly 273, 387
earrings 447
ears 8, 98, 118, 190, 194, 197, 201, 219, 231, 256, 334, 376, 391, 393, 395, 407, 448, 475, 477, 481, 499, 520, 529, 546, 561, 564, 582, 606
earth's 409
eased 100
eases 279, 419
easier 6, 112, 136, 164, 182, 252, 278, 289, 291, 293, 319, 437, 469, 528, 539, 554, 601, 607
eaters 3
eavesdropping 574
ebbs 489, 518, 567
echoes 390
echoing 489, 491, 543, 561
ecstatically 186
edges 27, 33, 42, 58, 106, 269, 316, 516, 536, 604
edited 236, 461
editing 285, 377, 458

Editorial Director 608
editors 299, 608
educating 609
Education Center 410
eerily 125, 176, 406
effacing 528
effectively 151, 187, 312, 454
efficiently 76
Effie 25, 26, 40, 41, 42, 50, 54, 56, 57, 58, 61, 62, 64, 65, 66, 68, 71, 73, 166, 184, 185, 186, 190, 196, 199, 220, 222, 223, 224, 226, 227, 228, 229, 232, 235, 236, 237, 240, 243, 245, 265, 268, 284, 294, 295, 296, 297, 298, 299, 310, 311, 312, 314, 318, 322, 323, 324, 327, 332, 497, 507, 571, 594, 596, 598
Effie Trinket 4, 10, 11, 12, 13, 14, 15, 23, 24, 25, 26, 30, 40, 41, 58, 166, 193, 199, 218, 219, 387, 497, 571, 585, 594
Effie Trinket's 25, 30, 40, 220, 440
Effie's 41, 57, 61, 65, 66, 186, 190, 219, 225, 283, 292, 311, 312
effortlessly 329, 335, 608
efforts 74, 155, 330, 342, 373, 385
eggs 28, 30, 47, 111, 203, 215, 312, 603, 605
eighteen age of 7
elaborately 242
elbows 48, 163, 311, 403, 424, 599
electrified 3, 275, 284
electrifying 393
electrocuted 277, 384, 437
electrocution 276
elevations 510
elevators 50, 55, 71, 309, 484, 511, 599
elevator's 533
elicited 231
eliminated 77, 121
eliminating 182, 188, 384, 597
Elizabeth 608
Ellie Berger 608
elongating 261
else's 158, 165, 573, 574
eludes 74
emanates 330
emanating 149, 457
embarrassed 18, 30, 34, 73, 109, 291
embarrasses 445
embedded 124, 400, 404
embellishments 573
embers 304, 604
emboldened 335

Embraced		503
embraces		237, 295, 308
embroidered		26, 239, 567
embryos		405
emerges		164, 457, 569
emerging		226, 453, 560
emerging	sense of	488
emits	480	
emitting		552
emotion	wave of	450
emotionally		158
emotionless		15
emotions		22, 71, 84, 88, 150, 153, 205, 264, 304, 329, 346, 516
emphatically		278
empowered		332
emptied		17, 255, 263, 289
empties		53, 54, 138
emptiness		186, 341, 470, 516, 599
emptying		376, 582
encased		32, 282
encases		359, 548
encasing		219, 447, 516
encircled		103
encircles		231, 529
encloses		78, 376
enclosing		3, 74
encompasses		386
encountered		13, 247, 335, 409, 564
encountering		325
encounters		14, 301
encouraged		95, 330
encouraging		146, 559
encouragingly		34, 68, 70
encroaching		10
endangered		212
Endangering		499
endearments		275
endings		573
endlessly		75
endlessness		227
enemies		24, 61, 81, 100, 101, 106, 128, 132, 346, 432, 444, 445, 493, 503, 509, 513, 519, 575, 597
enemy's		503
energized		93
enfolded		504

enfolding	237
enforced	227
enforcers	203
engineered	76, 609
engraved	343
engrossed	218
engulfed	39, 65, 328
engulfing	93
engulfs	180
enhancement	569
enhancements	433
enjoyed	28, 308
enjoying	223, 255, 361
enlarged	358
Enobaria	314, 318, 323, 327, 331, 337, 338, 340, 370, 382, 383, 385, 390, 393, 394, 396, 398, 423, 432, 446, 596, 597
Enobaria's	370, 371, 372, 373, 393
enraged	172, 440
ensnaring	433
ensuring	117
entails	487
entangled	124, 392
entered	7, 8, 9, 122, 303, 321, 447, 547
entering	202, 556
enters	20, 34, 65, 124, 261, 427, 517, 533, 596
entertainers	211
enthusiastically	40
entitled	28, 202, 476
entourages	71
Entranced	359
entrances	503, 504, 508, 510
entreaties	400
entries	7, 8, 27
entwined	225, 319
entwining	157, 392
enveloped	324
envelopes	287
enveloping	419
envelops	604
envied	67
enviously	187
environmental	474
EPILOGUE ACKNOWLEDGMENTS	611
episodes	554
equals	138, 157, 429

equipped	214, 302, 534, 535
eradicated	102
eradicates	361
erases	449
erasing	100, 180
ermissions	609
erupted	262
erupts	301, 388
escaped	130, 275, 357, 402, 403, 404, 405, 421, 500, 556, 595
escapees	270
escapes	176, 257, 412, 534
escaping	152, 227, 280, 396, 398, 561
escorted	294
escorts	193, 243, 465
essentially	16, 37, 62, 356, 387, 425
established	194, 503
et	519
Euh	136
Euuuh	136
evacuated	405, 567
evacuating	552
evading	358
evasively	158, 488, 514
evening's	9, 90, 235
events	29, 108, 129, 191, 211, 234, 269, 275, 303, 389, 402, 474, 475, 497, 512, 549, 571
Everdeen	70, 534, 596
Everdeens	420
Everdeen's	556
everybody's	517
everyone's	57, 69, 146, 195, 224, 225, 266, 313, 321, 327, 329, 332, 381, 439, 451, 466, 500, 509, 550, 564, 582
Everything's	125
evils	177
evolved	362
exaggerating	403
examined	328
examines	209, 210, 315, 386, 455, 506, 550
examining	32, 95, 278, 324, 348, 361, 391, 476
exasperated	160
exceeded	384
exceeds	412, 510
excels	52
Except Cinna	37
Except Enobaria	494

Except Gale	582	
Except I'd	126	
exceptions	51	
exchanged	168, 212, 239, 421	
exchanges	462, 467, 473, 532, 544	
exchanging	513, 574	
excitedly	449, 520	
excitement	glint of	111
exclaims	109	
exclamations	435	
excluded	383	
exclusively	24, 40, 410	
excused	396, 483, 498	
excuses	599	
executed	3, 182, 208, 231, 288, 444, 469, 497, 573	
executing	524	
executing	privilege of	572
exempted	474	
exercises	282, 293, 525, 546	
exhalations	561	
exhales	480	
exhausted	81, 89, 111, 140, 171, 217, 268, 284, 303, 350, 359, 431, 484, 497	
exhausting	24, 383, 543	
exhilarating	40	
existed	104, 280, 374, 404, 486, 504, 517	
existing	287, 288, 362, 547, 584	
exists	274, 569	
exits	424, 529	
exoneration	601	
expectantly	44, 142	
expectations	35, 221, 384, 510, 519, 586	
expected	15, 35, 145, 226, 241, 249, 292, 314, 368, 382, 410, 415, 422, 436, 447, 483, 511, 560, 577	
expects	178, 577	
experiencing	321	
experiments	513	
expertly	123	
experts	51, 328	
explained	439, 544	
explaining	315, 393, 507, 533	
explains	116, 385, 386, 415, 424, 437, 438, 475, 491, 519	
explanations	123	
exploded	272	
explodes	5, 47, 331, 394, 499	
exploding	591	

exploited 575

explosions 118, 119, 394, 453, 456, 510, 552

explosions chain of 553

explosives 116, 408, 437, 479, 565, 588

expressionless 197

expressions 255, 381, 437, 509

expression's 457

exquisitely 153

extending 424, 426

extends 231, 581, 584

exteriors 539

extinguished 92, 439

extinguishes 39, 455

extinguishing 305

extremes 516

extricating 166

exudes 204

eyebrows 33, 46, 57, 157, 169, 181, 187, 214, 216, 217, 238, 247, 259, 263, 300, 304, 334, 385, 412, 421, 432, 466, 518, 534

eyeing 326

eyelashes 260, 281

eyelids 59, 67, 74, 237, 279, 300, 307, 322, 361, 371, 395

eyeliner 35, 218

eye's 255

eyes|Foxface 176

fabricated 157, 557, 572

fabrics 218, 283, 520

facade 228, 452

faced 25, 42, 68, 76, 83, 191, 267, 369, 457, 567, 576

facedown 255, 354

faces| 378

faceup 403

facing prospect of 598

factly 289, 435

factories 36, 116, 236, 271

faculties 133

faded 231, 452, 506, 551

fades 83, 147, 213, 311, 553, 603, 605

failed 33, 138, 182, 192, 237, 239, 341, 393, 396, 409, 442, 463, 507, 508, 557

fails 333, 342, 385, 425, 573, 579

fainted 187

fainting 321

faintly 273, 321, 393

faking 215

falling 16, 52, 67, 103, 127, 225, 234, 276, 337, 342, 353, 366, 458, 461, 514, 546 falling   sensation of   277

falls   4, 11, 15, 26, 29, 65, 68, 73, 77, 81, 83, 89, 110, 119, 124, 174, 178, 179, 188, 292, 301, 309, 353, 359, 374, 406, 407, 457, 473, 506, 513, 514, 569, 583, 587, 588

families   5, 6, 48, 60, 120, 143, 199, 200, 214, 229, 230, 233, 244, 247, 251, 258, 259, 266, 308, 330, 420, 503, 573

family's   51, 59, 218, 222, 456, 498, 536, 606

fanged   207

fangs   284, 357, 358

fans   308, 585

fantasizing   368

fantastical   384

fared   135

faring   194

farms   420

fascinated   94, 304, 406, 493

fashioned   24, 327, 445

fashions   35, 344

fastened   60

fastens   77, 179, 431, 601

faster   79, 92, 297, 351, 380, 391, 422, 453, 562

fastest   389

fatalities   81, 147

fates   222

fathers   509

father's   5, 16, 22, 27, 28, 40, 60, 95, 104, 105, 160, 169, 201, 214, 245, 293, 364, 369, 405, 408, 411, 479, 498, 603, 606

favorites   38, 203, 286, 293

favors   157, 536

Fearing   120

fears   331, 395

feasted   29

Feasts   147

features   4, 42, 65, 102, 120, 152, 206, 495, 536, 565

featuring   425

feeds   154

feelings   168, 190, 194, 197, 210, 424, 477, 521, 551, 566, 575

feels   6, 27, 30, 33, 44, 47, 62, 74, 77, 100, 141, 150, 175, 185, 193, 196, 247, 257, 284, 289, 298, 323, 324, 326, 327, 357, 380, 399, 408, 426, 442, 462, 481, 482, 531, 541, 546, 589, 608

fees   609

feet   stampede of   91

female| 287

fenced   429

fences   284

ferreted   587

fervently   395
festering   smell of   135
festivities   222, 520
festooned   392
feverishly   183
fever's   144
fi   609
fiancé   248
fiancée   254, 543
fiancé's   248
fibers   392
fiddles   325, 377
fidgeting   65, 186
fields   227, 236, 316, 385
fiercely   112, 259, 325
Fiftieth Hunger Games   299
fighters   31, 313, 368, 513, 556
fighting   13, 23, 25, 33, 51, 54, 81, 85, 103, 132, 141, 169, 180, 250, 258, 262, 267, 293, 298, 315, 323, 327, 335, 336, 340, 375, 399, 415, 460, 473, 479, 487, 515, 518, 524, 526, 531, 532, 536, 550, 567, 571
Fighting Cato   130
fighting's   81, 502, 513
fights   92, 566
figures   75, 227, 339, 340, 362, 375, 395, 426
filed   184
filled   18, 23, 24, 27, 47, 51, 71, 93, 104, 132, 148, 151, 183, 211, 232, 239, 240, 245, 256, 257, 270, 291, 295, 347, 360, 365, 375, 404, 413, 436, 469, 555, 568
filling   pleasure of   241
fills   78, 86, 116, 118, 188, 209, 231, 251, 258, 259, 263, 316, 394, 440, 457, 479, 544, 577, 578
filmed   469, 531, 605
filming   206, 219, 447, 450, 544
filmmakers   192
films   466
filters   240
Finally Cinna   218
Finally Finnick   327
Finally Haymitch   265
Finally I'm   312
Finally Peeta   302
findings   386
fine   opposite of   480
finest   82
fingernails   58, 81, 95, 261, 360, 398, 531, 600
fingers   2, 14, 17, 19, 25, 28, 30, 31, 34, 35, 39, 42, 58, 59, 64, 78, 83, 91, 93, 94, 100,

102, 106, 108, 113, 118, 120, 122, 126, 137, 138, 143, 148, 150, 157, 169, 174, 178, 179, 180, 182, 183, 184, 202, 205, 212, 214, 223, 225, 231, 238, 243, 246, 248, 256, 259, 261, 269, 271, 277, 279, 306, 311, 314, 320, 321, 322, 325, 326, 331, 333, 341, 342, 349, 351, 354, 355, 356, 357, 359, 367, 371, 381, 395, 396, 412, 418, 432, 433, 434, 443, 448, 449, 470, 471, 477, 481, 484, 485, 493, 495, 498, 505, 511, 516, 521, 534, 543, 545, 559, 569, 571, 579, 582, 584, 586

fingertips   91, 214, 529
finishes   19, 73, 110, 226, 315, 316, 492, 508, 530, 534, 560, 578
finishing   25, 228, 251, 314, 396
Finnick   296, 305, 306, 307, 309, 311, 312, 313, 314, 315, 318, 319, 323, 328, 332, 336, 337, 338, 339, 340, 341, 342, 343, 344, 345, 346, 347, 348, 349, 350, 351, 352, 353, 354, 355, 356, 357, 358, 359, 360, 361, 362, 363, 365, 366, 367, 368, 369, 370, 371, 372, 373, 374, 375, 376, 377, 378, 379, 381, 383, 384, 385, 386, 387, 388, 390, 391, 393, 396, 397, 398, 399, 406, 407, 422, 431, 432, 437, 439, 440, 443, 444, 460, 461, 462, 463, 472, 473, 474, 475, 483, 484, 485, 487, 488, 489, 490, 491, 492, 493, 494, 507, 519, 520, 522, 527, 528, 529, 531, 533, 534, 535, 536, 537, 539, 543, 544, 548, 550, 552, 553, 555, 556, 557, 562, 563, 566, 568, 572, 573, 592, 597

Finnick Odair   305, 307, 342, 361, 406, 445, 491
Finnick Odair's   305, 399
Finnick   photo of   607
Finnick   sight of   341
Finnicks   492
Finnick's   313, 320, 339, 340, 341, 342, 352, 353, 355, 356, 360, 362, 364, 365, 371, 374, 379, 382, 387, 392, 397, 399, 432, 437, 461, 465, 483, 485, 491, 492, 493, 494, 508, 528, 534, 537, 543, 547, 558
Finnick's   color of   585, 606
Finnick's   thud of   358
Fire Girl   153
fire   wall of   91, 93
firearms   437, 581
fireballs   93, 192
firebombing   466, 603
firebombs   400, 402, 576
fired   94, 113, 163, 180, 391, 593
firefight   533
Firefighters   553
fireflies   44
firelight   38, 39, 98
fireplaces   239
fires   10, 22, 52, 86, 102, 103, 125, 169, 170, 180, 250, 304, 315, 329, 359, 362, 403, 404, 510
fire's   417, 453
firestorm   403
firmer   114
firmly   133, 309, 340, 434, 452, 535, 538, 546, 592
fished   211

fishhooks 319, 338

fissures 483

fistful 183, 278, 433

fists 12, 79, 119, 191, 311, 355, 487, 530

fits 77, 100, 269, 443

Five Career Tributes 84

fixated 53, 55, 281, 308, 377, 454

fixedly 476

fixes 21, 220, 334, 400, 449

flagrantly 459

flags 207

flailing 97, 338, 483

flakes 604

flamboyantly 239

flame balls of 585

flame feathers of 585

flames 18, 38, 39, 42, 59, 69, 74, 84, 92, 93, 95, 210, 239, 266, 304, 312, 328, 336, 394, 398, 403, 404, 405, 439, 441, 453, 454, 455, 457, 458, 500, 556, 595, 596, 603

flames wall of 94

flanked 454

flaps 582

flares 518, 552

flashbacks 607

flashes 193, 212, 253, 281

flashlights 83, 85, 551

flasks 149

flatly 8, 298, 323, 377, 423

flattened 136, 407, 416, 526, 569, 606

flattening 396, 546

flattens 337, 348

flaunted 190, 212

flaunting 362

Flavius 34, 186, 187, 190, 216, 217, 223, 240, 282, 283, 303, 325, 427, 431, 434, 594, 595

Flavius's 426, 428, 435

flawless 55, 338, 412, 433, 593

flawlessly 237

flaws 265

fleas 2

flecks 537

fleeing 45, 64, 153, 271, 284, 288, 576, 579

flesh nest of 563

flesh ring of 526

flexes 248, 579

flickered 424, 571

flickering 39, 106, 187, 304, 346, 479, 510, 513, 556, 570
flickers 39, 290, 329, 337, 457
flickery 328
flicking 312
flicks 203, 570, 598
flies 254, 263, 273, 282, 302, 347, 391, 403, 449, 510, 579, 583
flinches 427
flinging 168, 357
flings 152, 365
flipped 542
flipping 563
flips 152, 242, 249, 297, 418, 453, 508
flirting 555
floated 28
flocks 505
flooding 388
floods 32, 202, 214, 240, 366, 503
floorboards 266
floored 38
floors 206, 245, 284, 426
flops 176, 395
flowed 349
flowers 27, 35, 38, 52, 71, 91, 126, 127, 128, 149, 152, 192, 196, 197, 209, 214, 229, 230, 231, 232, 300, 319, 322, 325, 348, 387, 407, 408, 410, 437, 471, 486, 516, 517, 521, 604
flows 71, 475
fluffed 567
flurries 568
flushed 257, 312, 452, 477, 604
flushes 145, 151, 413
fluttered 125
fluttering 36
flutters 68
focused 126, 365, 454, 498, 499
focuses 191
focusing 290, 434, 466
fog wall of 351, 353, 368
fogginess 504
folded 511
folding 420, 477, 582
folds 330, 424
followed 18, 106, 119, 129, 170, 188, 192, 207, 210, 214, 222, 247, 272, 286, 291, 348, 420, 424, 442, 458, 478, 537, 544, 555, 573
following| 415
follows 73, 85, 89, 193, 252, 337, 356, 370, 412, 419, 427, 433, 455, 477, 498,

508, 543, 552, 573, 598, 603

food   excess of   519
food   scraps of   252
food   smell of   360
food   vats of   420
foodladen   317
foods   211
food's   5, 45, 112, 170, 271
fooled   170
fooling   385, 393, 478
foolishly   53, 61, 160
foolishness   248, 282
fools   16, 146, 591
footage   quality of   544
footfalls   173
footprints   206, 268, 551
footsteps   69, 82, 103, 186, 224, 291, 336, 346, 390, 403, 462, 477, 489, 548
for|and   337
for|everything   478
for|for   269
for|my   470
for|what   576
forages   112
forays   571
forbids   414
forcefully   454, 581
forces   32, 245, 301, 313, 376, 399, 410, 441, 512, 513, 538, 548, 586
forcing   11, 17, 147, 151, 231, 259, 278, 484
forearms   437, 595
forehead's   137
foreseen   94
forests   79, 236
forgettable   72
forgetting   90, 163, 379, 400
forgivable   260
forgives   515
formed   61, 85, 338, 404, 412, 504, 585, 602
forming   12, 33, 89, 174, 230, 326, 328, 448, 476, 495, 521
forms   16, 327, 539, 580, 582
formulated   99
forties   444
fortifications   507
fortified   504, 514
Fortifying   519
fortunately   14, 91, 101, 118, 141, 150, 168, 228, 229, 364, 371, 410, 451, 532, 555,

568, 607

fortunes 73

Forty Seven 478

foundations 247

fourhour 271

fours 152, 564

fourteen age of 296

Foxface 84, 116, 120, 121, 128, 131, 139, 141, 147, 149, 150, 152, 154, 163, 169, 170, 171, 172, 174, 177

Foxface's 116, 117, 169

fractured 120

fragmenting 120

framed 581

frantically 93, 222, 368, 371, 408, 454, 561, 565, 585

freaks 430, 517

freedoms 221

freeing 124, 182

frees 336, 377, 390, 550

freezes 183, 333, 408, 560

fresh glint of 205

fresh smell of 17

freshly 533

frets 236

Friday 142

friendliest 43

friends 6, 7, 15, 18, 40, 43, 50, 54, 61, 62, 112, 120, 129, 165, 204, 214, 225, 233, 244, 254, 260, 262, 265, 280, 288, 296, 297, 303, 313, 314, 315, 317, 318, 323, 327, 330, 332, 339, 361, 367, 376, 377, 380, 397, 440, 444, 448, 457, 489, 500, 501, 502, 525, 529, 531, 533, 535, 560, 562, 573, 574, 599, 609

friendship pressure of 184

fries 346

frightening 28, 67, 496, 499, 565, 607

frightens 43, 118, 472, 478

frilly 73, 183

frocks 304

frogs 130

frowned 143

frowning 345, 430, 448, 604

frowns 62, 146, 203, 242, 263, 290, 333, 343, 432, 508, 558

fruits 239

frustrates 558

frying 48, 577

fueled 93, 547

fulfilled 399

fullness 424

Fulvia   422, 423, 424, 425, 426, 428, 433, 434, 439, 440, 441, 459, 460, 462, 492
Fulvia Cardew   406, 410, 445, 457
Fulvia's   425, 427, 434, 440, 441, 459, 465
fumbles   94
fumbling   91, 255, 417
fumes   30, 220, 270, 457, 548, 551, 593
functioning   367
funerals   14
funneled   503, 525
funnier   528
fur   layer of   575
furiously   182
furrowing   459
furs   244, 569, 572, 587
fussing   314
future   sort of   480
gadgets   41, 283, 434
gagging   563
gags   175
gained   152, 402, 517
gaining   398, 531
Gale Hawthorne   199
Gale   pictures of   527
Gale   sight of   421
Gale| 60
Gale'd   266
Gale's   5, 7, 8, 14, 60, 61, 105, 125, 142, 148, 157, 165, 201, 211, 212, 215, 222, 241, 247, 248, 249, 250, 253, 254, 255, 256, 257, 261, 263, 271, 290, 295, 375, 403, 404, 407, 408, 411, 417, 423, 426, 429, 430, 435, 438, 448, 452, 454, 455, 463, 464, 466, 470, 489, 498, 499, 505, 506, 510, 512, 518, 524, 528, 530, 546, 563, 566, 567, 570, 571, 575, 580, 590, 605, 607
Gale's   pressure of   212
Gale's   sizzle of   263
gallons   551
Gamemaker   69, 92, 93, 316, 366, 383, 395, 434, 496, 520
Gamemakers   48, 49, 52, 54, 55, 56, 57, 58, 65, 66, 67, 68, 69, 74, 76, 88, 92, 93, 94, 101, 108, 110, 111, 117, 119, 129, 130, 133, 138, 141, 146, 148, 152, 158, 164, 172, 173, 179, 181, 182, 187, 188, 189, 191, 208, 241, 316, 317, 319, 320, 321, 343, 354, 360, 370, 374, 388, 394, 433, 534
Gamemaker's   358
games   1, 13, 23, 25, 26, 35, 37, 38, 40, 43, 44, 46, 47, 56, 61, 70, 73, 74, 75, 77, 84, 85, 92, 102, 105, 110, 111, 114, 115, 117, 125, 126, 128, 130, 131, 135, 140, 148, 156, 157, 161, 162, 166, 173, 179, 183, 187, 188, 189, 190, 191, 196, 197, 199, 200, 202, 203, 204, 210, 211, 215, 216, 217, 218, 219, 221, 222, 225, 226, 230, 237, 239, 242, 244, 249, 260, 262, 268, 274, 281, 286, 288, 290, 292, 293, 295, 296, 297, 298, 300, 303, 306, 308, 310, 312, 313, 317, 320, 323, 327, 330, 331, 332, 333, 335, 340, 344, 345, 347, 351, 354, 367, 369, 373, 376, 377, 378,

379, 380, 381, 382, 385, 394, 395, 397, 398, 399, 400, 406, 407, 413, 417, 418, 425, 429, 433, 458, 460, 480, 483, 490, 507, 512, 515, 528, 533, 535, 538, 549, 556, 557, 570, 571, 572, 575, 595, 597, 598, 608, 610

Games Headquarters 73
gamey 347
gaping 55, 95, 117, 173, 177, 434, 435, 566, 581
garbled 318, 515
garden outlines of 16
gardens 239
gargling 355
garments 78, 569, 594, 604
garnered 609
garroting 367
gashes 175, 334
gasping 92, 175, 328, 354, 358, 371, 488, 497
gasps 57, 109, 229, 520
gates 3, 429
gathered 24, 28, 51, 53, 108, 120, 123, 144, 170, 188, 211, 327, 338, 411, 547
gathers 170, 386
gawking 33
gazes 316, 432
gazing 138
gel's 551
gems 65, 94, 223
generated 444
generates 222, 455
generations 237, 423
generators 485
generously 167
genetically 24, 208, 246, 486
gentlemen 78, 182, 334
gentlemen| 534
gentler 250, 416
gentlest 599
gently 38, 64, 66, 70, 87, 100, 104, 124, 134, 137, 153, 182, 195, 235, 254, 257, 325, 330, 358, 376, 382, 457, 470, 483, 560, 570
genuinely 21, 39, 52, 90, 117, 270, 310, 403, 441, 456, 478, 500, 506
gestures 38, 62, 206, 329, 354, 466, 549, 569
gesturing 363, 547
getting 7, 21, 39, 46, 47, 75, 83, 92, 111, 120, 130, 132, 138, 156, 157, 158, 194, 196, 203, 206, 218, 220, 223, 228, 252, 255, 276, 278, 281, 283, 284, 288, 303, 308, 315, 318, 321, 332, 338, 363, 373, 375, 377; 396, 413, 420, 424, 434, 451, 457, 476, 488, 505, 518, 522, 527, 532, 533, 537, 545, 571, 595, 608
Getting Gale 416
Getting Mags 367

ghosts 603
giants 68
giddiness 144, 494
gift|it 230
gifts 11, 21, 26, 73, 138, 140, 162, 232, 243, 247, 306, 348, 361, 388, 584
gifts flow of 89
giggles 9, 112, 435
giggling 69, 72, 73, 278
girls 6, 10, 12, 46, 51, 79, 85, 109, 159, 161, 187, 223, 229, 244, 294, 299, 389, 491, 502, 506
girl's 13, 42, 45, 123, 259, 269
Girls 20
Girl's 143
giver 39, 418
giving 44, 46, 60, 70, 77, 87, 143, 144, 165, 176, 194, 205, 222, 233, 236, 238, 264, 265, 316, 322, 326, 327, 329, 341, 355, 367, 380, 440, 454, 459, 523, 529, 539, 547, 579, 606
glanced 17
glances 51, 254, 257, 342, 365, 435, 523
glancing 99, 191, 243, 307, 432, 584
glassed 439
gleaming 555
gleams 172
gleefully 14
glides 348
Glimmer's 103, 105, 113, 128, 174, 226, 320, 376
glimpses 307, 507
glinting 353
glints 149, 514
glistening 32, 336, 387, 596
glittering 37
gloomily 248
gloppy 107
glorified 286, 539
gloved 183, 269, 312, 583, 605
gloves 153, 219, 245, 247, 248, 251, 252, 268, 327, 334, 478
glowering 176
glows 184, 187, 455
glued 39, 133, 305, 319, 351, 364, 379, 548, 590
glues 76
glumly 384
gnats 539
gnawed 467
gnaws 297, 367
goat smell of 164
goats 143, 239

Goat's 35
gobbled 154
gold flecks of 35
gold thread of 394
goodbyes 450, 598
gorging 105
gorging days of 81
government's 603
gowns 283, 285, 286, 304, 330, 520
grabbed 27, 79, 256, 511
grabs 14, 38, 72, 151, 166, 216, 250, 282, 327, 521
gracefully 92
graciously 226
grades 317
gradually 6, 121, 164, 304, 356, 586
grafts 587
grandkids 109
granted 216, 405, 411, 423, 432, 482, 524, 592, 607, 609
grapes 42, 344, 459
grasps 472
grasses 156, 215
gratefully 43, 139, 202
gratified 22
graying 245
grazed 565
greased 357
Greasy Sae 6, 7, 142, 148, 202, 204, 265, 267, 431, 440, 507, 521, 528, 603, 604, 606
Greasy Sae's 25, 109, 203, 255, 310, 507, 603
Greeks 609
greens 5, 6, 8, 9, 27, 28, 32, 42, 108, 112, 120, 142, 170, 172
greeted 214
Greetings 181
greets 395, 472
Gregor 609
grieved 511
grieving 15, 503
grimacing 546
grime layer of 531
grimly 22, 41, 155, 223, 437, 453
grimmer 479
grimness 9
grinding 116, 144, 546
grinds 100
grinning 97, 282, 309, 494
grins 36, 336, 416, 517, 525, 541

gripped	350
grips	145, 310, 321, 332, 339, 359, 462
gritted	37, 134, 259
gritting	526
groaning	107
groans	355
grocer's	17
groggily	464
groomed	41, 462, 589
grooms	327
groosling	107, 121, 122, 135, 138, 139, 141, 154, 156
groosling leg of	271
grooslings	128
groosling's	156
grossly	543
grouchily	185, 363
groundbreaking	609
grounded	538
grounds	166, 204
ground's	276, 583
growling	6, 97, 122, 176, 348
growls	66, 178, 558
grows	54, 126, 221, 310, 346, 357, 380, 586
grubbiness	172
grudgingly	60
gruffly	13, 72, 152, 332
grumbling	17, 88
grunts	348
guaranteed	87, 173, 222
guaranteeing	178
guarantees	569
guarding	2, 26, 151, 237, 389, 606
guards	56, 186, 227, 294, 386, 396, 415, 418, 429, 477, 529, 530, 531, 536, 540, 543, 545, 559, 588, 589, 594, 598, 599
guard's	426, 427, 599
Guards	429, 598
Guess I'd	183
guess|back	197
guessed	116, 208, 344, 347, 412
guessing	7, 88, 95, 103, 117, 164, 229, 298, 312, 562, 570
guests	67, 239, 288, 520, 521
guffaws	58
guided	598, 608
guides	76, 186, 231, 237, 332, 428, 474, 578, 579
guilt admission of	464

guiltily	75
gulps	289, 350, 365, 367, 485
gums	339
gunfire's	513
guns	76, 265, 281, 294, 452, 471, 499, 511, 514, 515, 526, 544, 545, 549, 551, 562, 581, 588, 589
gurgling	598
gurney	494
gushes	13
gushing	375
guts	79, 246, 481
gutted	87
gutting	346
guys	537
guy's	242
habits	587, 605
hackles	357
haggling	6
hair|it	159
hairband	188, 189, 228
haired	207, 296
hairs	351
hair's	188, 217, 567
halls	67, 232, 415, 494, 533
hallucinating	402
hallucinations	99, 102, 496
hallucinations|	174
hallways	312, 588
halted	589
haltingly	160, 501
hammers	184, 334, 597
hammocks	318
hampered	175
hand|this	122
handbags	579
handcuffed	19
handcuffs	571, 575
handedly	8
handfuls	28, 31, 170, 355, 466, 536
handheld	429, 539
handing	160, 554
handled	291
handouts	4
handpicked	537
handwritten	27

hanged 272, 275

hangers 593

Hanging Tree 467, 468, 469, 471, 493, 512, 554, 586

hangs 12, 65, 98, 99, 113, 116, 176, 253, 276, 343, 375, 408, 413, 427, 448, 551, 584, 607

happened 15, 18, 23, 45, 57, 58, 69, 105, 109, 114, 123, 129, 142, 152, 155, 159, 161, 163, 168, 210, 211, 212, 225, 226, 231, 232, 235, 236, 246, 248, 250, 254, 255, 256, 258, 264, 275, 279, 284, 286, 306, 332, 340, 349, 356, 358, 363, 390, 397, 400, 404, 415, 427, 430, 461, 469, 492, 496, 497, 501, 507, 515, 521, 523, 530, 535, 542, 544, 551, 553, 560, 572, 578, 588, 591, 592, 595, 606, 607

happens 14, 20, 51, 81, 100, 116, 118, 134, 140, 172, 180, 185, 192, 222, 231, 237, 321, 323, 331, 350, 353, 357, 362, 366, 376, 378, 384, 425, 428, 442, 554, 563, 566, 576, 584, 600

happier 389, 517

happiest 141

Happy Hunger Games 5, 11

hardens 405, 414

harder 82, 109, 148, 179, 205, 262, 282, 315, 320, 341, 343, 348, 354, 389, 419, 433, 495, 513, 582, 603

hardest 155, 497

hardships 234, 267, 283

harm's 407

harnessing 384

harried 332

harshly 13, 54, 98, 227, 251, 269, 363

Harvest Festival 204, 243, 244, 245, 247

harvested 27, 28

harvesting 59

hastens 326

hastily 490, 511, 552, 568, 579

hatched 448

hated 16, 22, 29, 86, 95, 201, 211, 293, 376, 485, 530, 585, 586

hates 2, 89, 161, 290, 365, 402, 421, 530, 587

hating 50, 153, 187, 197, 506

hats 36, 227, 329

hauled 45, 503

hauling 23, 352, 451, 477, 566, 583

hauls 353, 463

hauntingly 25

haunts 412, 457

hawks 42

Hawthornes 420, 485

Haymitch 11, 14, 20, 26, 27, 30, 31, 32, 33, 34, 37, 40, 41, 42, 43, 45, 47, 48, 49, 50, 53, 54, 56, 57, 58, 61, 62, 63, 64, 65, 66, 69, 71, 72, 73, 74, 76, 78, 79, 86, 89, 90, 100, 107, 127, 136, 137, 138, 140, 146, 155, 156, 157, 158, 159, 160, 161, 162, 165, 171, 185, 186, 187,

188, 189, 191, 193, 194, 195, 196, 197, 203, 204, 205, 206, 215, 217, 218, 220, 221, 222, 223, 224, 225, 226, 232, 233, 234, 235, 236, 237, 238, 243, 248, 249, 250, 252, 254, 255, 256, 257, 258, 259, 261, 263, 264, 265, 267, 278, 282, 284, 285, 287, 288, 289, 290, 291, 292, 293, 294, 295, 296, 297, 298, 299, 300, 301, 302, 303, 305, 307, 308, 309, 310, 311, 312, 313, 314, 315, 317, 318, 319, 321, 322, 323, 324, 326, 327, 330, 332, 333, 336, 338, 340, 344, 346, 348, 350, 358, 360, 365, 373, 375, 378, 379, 380, 385, 394, 397, 398, 399, 400, 414, 419, 440, 441, 442, 443, 445, 446, 451, 454, 457, 459, 460, 461, 465, 473, 474, 481, 484, 486, 487, 488, 489, 490, 491, 492, 493, 494, 495, 496, 497, 499, 500, 501, 502, 504, 505, 510, 511, 512, 513, 514, 515, 519, 521, 522, 523, 524, 527, 528, 535, 542, 543, 553, 586, 587, 588, 589, 592, 593, 594, 596, 597, 601, 602, 603, 606, 607

Haymitch Abernathy   11, 217, 298, 412, 414
Haymitch I'll   313
Haymitch   image of   161
Haymitch   sight of   460
Haymitch| 325
Haymitch|well   161
Haymitch's   24, 26, 31, 50, 51, 53, 76, 80, 82, 146, 160, 162, 186, 188, 190, 204, 205, 220, 226, 229, 267, 289, 292, 293, 294, 297, 298, 299, 300, 302, 310, 311, 333, 336, 340, 348, 361, 394, 398, 400, 440, 443, 451, 452, 459, 473, 474, 488, 489, 494, 507, 511, 513, 514, 523, 542, 603

Haymitch's Quell   304
Hazelle   201, 202, 204, 212, 223, 241, 247, 250, 251, 255, 257, 259, 266, 267, 284, 292, 435, 553

Hazelle's   259
he| 425
Head Gamemaker   208, 241, 242, 316, 320, 402, 451, 460, 471, 590
Head Office   426
Head Peacekeeper   28, 203, 254, 255, 257, 316, 404, 491, 577, 578
Head Peacekeeper Thread   277, 279, 294
head| 402
headaches   209, 244
headache's   421
headdresses   38, 39
headlamps   36, 304
head's   151, 290, 549
healed   78, 114, 197, 356, 456, 525
healer   140, 355, 570, 571
healers   5, 95
healer's   257
healthier   51, 420
heaping   165
heard   17, 28, 29, 40, 44, 45, 60, 85, 87, 102, 121, 127, 131, 133, 152, 161, 163, 203, 217, 232, 235, 240, 241, 244, 248, 250, 256, 263, 264, 278, 285, 287, 339, 360, 374, 376, 377, 380, 395, 406, 438, 451, 463, 465, 470, 475, 480, 495, 500, 512, 514, 521, 532
hearing   shock of   235, 440

hears 236, 585

heartbeats 404

heartlessly 17

heart's 274

heaters 41

heating 540

heavens 180

Heavensbee 396

heavier 97, 352

heaviest 81

heaving 391

he'd 16, 27, 48, 59, 60, 61, 76, 79, 86, 131, 132, 138, 148, 155, 167, 177, 195, 197, 200, 204, 208, 211, 215, 218, 225, 254, 256, 293, 296, 305, 306, 336, 347, 391, 394, 405, 417, 423, 469, 477, 496, 497, 504, 507, 522, 542, 550, 554, 572, 573, 578, 592, 602

hedges 301

heels 62, 67, 147, 175, 188, 212, 283, 324, 328, 342, 351, 364, 393, 571, 594, 606

hees 354

hefts 438

heightened 544

he'll 19, 31, 76, 90, 128, 132, 146, 147, 148, 151, 153, 158, 163, 166, 169, 170, 177, 178, 179, 218, 223, 251, 258, 265, 266, 268, 290, 292, 296, 298, 306, 318, 380, 396, 422, 453, 494, 497, 506, 540, 561, 573, 578, 583, 602

helmeted 564

helped 45, 49, 72, 95, 124, 152, 155, 242, 274, 355, 478

helplessly 124, 199, 461

helplessness 82

helps 19, 77, 96, 136, 149, 187, 279, 281, 326, 333, 343, 351, 409, 435, 443, 568, 594

her|tell 332

her|this 256

herbs 5, 19, 96, 144, 256, 258

herded 10, 404

herding 345

herds 227, 243

here's 8, 31, 63, 70, 142, 164, 238, 384, 540

he's 2, 6, 7, 11, 12, 13, 14, 15, 19, 20, 21, 23, 26, 27, 30, 31, 34, 36, 41, 43, 45, 46, 48, 50, 52, 53, 61, 63, 64, 65, 67, 68, 69, 72, 74, 75, 76, 79, 81, 86, 87, 89, 90, 98, 103, 110, 112, 114, 115, 128, 130, 131, 132, 133, 134, 135, 137, 138, 139, 140, 143, 145, 146, 147, 148, 149, 151, 152, 154, 156, 157, 158, 159, 160, 161, 162, 163, 164, 165, 166, 167, 168, 170, 171, 172, 173, 174, 175, 176, 178, 179, 180, 181, 186, 189, 190, 192, 194, 195, 197, 200, 202, 203, 206, 207, 208, 213, 215, 218, 220, 221, 223, 224, 225, 233, 241, 242, 243, 244, 248, 249, 250, 251, 252, 253, 254, 256, 261, 262, 266, 267, 278, 284, 285, 286, 289, 290, 291, 293, 294, 296, 297, 299, 300, 302, 303, 305, 306, 308, 309, 310, 313, 314, 316, 317, 320, 322, 323, 325, 328, 329, 330, 333, 334, 335, 336, 338, 339, 340, 341, 342, 350, 351, 352, 355, 356, 357, 360, 361, 364, 368, 369, 370, 371, 372, 373, 374, 375, 376, 377, 378, 389, 392, 393, 399, 403, 404, 405, 406, 407, 408, 414, 415, 416, 417, 420, 421, 422, 423, 425, 428, 430, 431, 434, 436, 437, 438,

440, 441, 443, 444, 449, 451, 455, 457, 458, 459, 463, 464, 465, 466, 467, 468, 469, 471, 472, 477, 478, 481, 482, 486, 487, 488, 489, 494, 495, 496, 497, 498, 504, 508, 509, 510, 514, 515, 519, 522, 523, 524, 527, 528, 530, 531, 532, 533, 535, 536, 540, 541, 546, 547, 548, 552, 553, 554, 559, 560, 561, 563, 570, 573, 577, 578, 587, 589, 590, 592, 593, 598, 601, 602, 603, 604, 605, 606

He's|he's   437
hesitates   70, 75, 229, 321, 350, 400, 483, 554
hesitating   61, 153, 565
hewn   475
hiccups   211
hides   105
highlighted   327
highlights   128, 191, 304, 472
hijacked   495, 499, 512, 523, 542, 547, 590
hijacking   496, 497, 542
hiking   62
hills   4, 14, 81, 124
him| 310
him|he   522
hindquarters   177
hinges   232, 426, 438
hinting   425
hints   284, 325
hips   184, 487
hisses   26, 103, 363, 390, 502, 536, 606
hits   48, 89, 93, 97, 137, 146, 149, 161, 162, 174, 176, 178, 209, 219, 221, 231, 236, 262, 305, 322, 334, 341, 344, 362, 365, 384, 386, 389, 452, 453, 458, 462, 478, 485, 486, 494, 533, 539, 546, 556, 557, 582, 600, 601
hitting   318, 334, 344, 351, 372, 381, 400, 523, 532, 582, 593
hoarsely   353, 427, 499, 536
hoarseness   495
Hob|that's   266
hobbled   158
hobbles   353
hobbling   175
hoisted   256
hoisting   347
hoists   255, 339
holding   tension of   483
holds   4, 10, 14, 21, 30, 33, 35, 39, 44, 55, 75, 101, 107, 109, 111, 128, 154, 182, 184, 192, 205, 207, 209, 213, 239, 240, 241, 247, 257, 258, 270, 271, 273, 288, 297, 302, 307, 326, 350, 360, 364, 376, 380, 387, 388, 400, 416, 418, 431, 435, 441, 446, 460, 489, 495, 506, 519, 527, 529, 538, 551, 555, 559, 574, 576, 579, 586, 589, 594, 595, 598, 606
holes   142, 148, 154, 358
holidays   520

hollering 11, 460

hollers 14, 286, 547

hollowly 180

hollowness 49

Holo 539, 541, 545, 546, 547, 548, 549, 550, 552, 556, 557, 559, 560, 562, 563, 564, 566, 567, 606

holographic 533

Holos 559

Holo's 539

home/prison 37

homes 67, 95, 264, 272, 285, 404, 448, 479, 563, 577

home's 601

Homes 537, 546, 547, 548, 549, 550, 551, 552, 553, 556, 557, 558, 564, 565, 572

honey color of 35

honeypot 510

honing 101

honors 555

hood's 96

hooking 130

hooting 69

hoots 85, 98

hoped 77, 275, 339, 459

hopelessly 124, 165, 183, 376, 482

hopelessness 15

hopes 117, 180, 274, 282, 342, 412, 415, 505

hoping 12, 14, 27, 31, 36, 47, 56, 60, 71, 74, 92, 97, 105, 123, 129, 138, 147, 148, 149, 161, 200, 277, 278, 279, 284, 285, 305, 330, 336, 346, 516, 523, 536, 537, 542, 589, 591, 592, 594

hopped 151

hops 26, 116, 466, 498

hormones 342

horns 75, 216

horrifies 479

horrifying 451, 461, 593

horrors 354, 463, 558, 602

horses 37, 39, 305, 485

hosed 428

hoses 553

hospitalized 499

hospitals 448

hosted 67

hosts 410, 577

hotter 132, 347

hours 3, 9, 18, 28, 30, 33, 36, 44, 60, 62, 64, 76, 80, 81, 83, 84, 91, 93, 112, 114, 123, 127, 133, 140, 147, 148, 158, 164, 165, 167, 170, 171, 179, 191, 193, 196, 199, 200, 211, 212,

220, 244, 247, 267, 268, 272, 277, 279, 283, 297, 304, 315, 347, 350, 360, 366, 368, 371, 378, 379, 383, 387, 408, 418, 422, 429, 439, 460, 461, 481, 484, 489, 491, 497, 498, 505, 508, 509, 512, 513, 525, 531, 559, 561, 562, 571, 572, 574, 588, 603, 606

hour's 224

Hours 508

housed 270, 438

houseful 46

houseguests 577, 580

houses 3, 29, 161, 204, 227, 241, 244, 255, 264, 287, 305, 402, 406, 415, 496, 503, 602

hovercraft exit of 503

hoverplane 453, 538

hoverplanes 404, 409, 451, 453, 510, 518, 538

How|how 58

How'd 365

howls 393, 409

How's 97, 210, 250, 279, 317, 505

How's Finnick 437

How's Gale 264

huddled 13, 15, 22, 61, 159, 311, 416, 432, 566, 584

huddles 434, 480

hues 32

hugging 20, 133, 163, 195, 299, 564, 581

hugs 186, 202, 214, 292, 411

human flow of 580

human stains of 428

humanity destruction of 462

humans 126, 142, 354, 386, 499

humiliated 55, 288

hummingbirds 436

humoring 173

hunched 3, 16, 229, 230, 493, 559, 569, 596

hunches 284

hunching 376, 452

hundreds 23, 44, 71, 81, 327, 405, 520, 538, 559, 567, 596

Hunger Games 1, 4, 11, 22, 32, 47, 52, 63, 64, 67, 78, 93, 94, 98, 99, 110, 120, 161, 178, 181, 182, 189, 190, 192, 193, 196, 199, 206, 207, 217, 248, 254, 270, 271, 282, 286, 287, 295, 297, 305, 323, 324, 334, 339, 394, 397, 402, 412, 421, 437, 445, 446, 456, 457, 467, 469, 496, 503, 515, 518, 519, 523, 534, 556, 569, 570, 587, 597, 599, 601, 607, 608, 609

Hunger Games Dedication Table 610

Hunger Games Trilogy 1

hunger effects of 100

hungover 292, 594

hungriest 258

hungrily 185

hunkered 453

hunted   95, 150, 156, 164, 168, 189, 211, 276, 362

hunters   45, 142, 599

hunter's   106, 120, 407

Hunting Cato   151

hunting   basics of   274

hunts   5, 196

hurled   553

hurray   117, 180

hurries   42, 73, 219, 232, 478, 492, 513

hurrying   59

hurting   94, 157, 258, 261, 283, 359, 430, 591, 594

hurts   20, 63, 78, 88, 166, 284, 399, 434, 486, 513, 521, 525, 593

husbands   511

hushed   9, 61, 86, 101, 112, 133, 250, 296, 322

hushing   192

hustled   440

hustles   245, 445, 447

hyperventilating   103

hysterically   13, 102, 240

I|I'm   136

I|well   305

ices   373

I'd   4, 12, 15, 16, 17, 18, 20, 27, 28, 35, 45, 46, 50, 53, 54, 56, 59, 60, 61, 68, 69, 85, 87, 88, 89, 90, 96, 100, 105, 108, 115, 116, 117, 118, 129, 130, 131, 132, 134, 136, 137, 142, 144, 145, 149, 151, 159, 161, 166, 167, 171, 173, 186, 200, 208, 211, 212, 215, 218, 222, 225, 234, 251, 265, 270, 276, 277, 280, 289, 292, 293, 295, 299, 306, 313, 314, 316, 317, 320, 324, 351, 358, 360, 361, 363, 368, 382, 383, 384, 386, 392, 428, 433, 435, 436, 438, 451, 452, 453, 465, 467, 483, 495, 496, 500, 507, 509, 511, 516, 530, 552, 576, 585, 589, 590, 599, 602

ideas   265, 316, 319, 499, 556

identically   66

identified   101, 568

identifies   552, 556

idiots   34, 279, 572

idly   143

if| 157

if|I   422

if|they   295

ifs   382

ignited   585

ignites   38, 119, 595

ignored   56, 108, 114, 125, 212, 309, 313, 314, 326, 459, 474, 510

ignores   68, 183, 254, 301, 344

ignoring   53, 57, 225, 285, 291, 302, 320, 522, 534

II   1, 70, 198, 269, 401, 473, 610, 611

III   1, 130, 198, 334, 401, 540, 610, 611

I'll 7, 13, 14, 20, 21, 22, 26, 29, 30, 32, 36, 37, 41, 43, 48, 53, 54, 56, 58, 62, 66, 67, 74, 75, 81, 82, 84, 85, 97, 99, 104, 106, 108, 112, 113, 121, 123, 131, 132, 133, 136, 140, 145, 146, 147, 149, 152, 154, 156, 158, 162, 163, 165, 168, 170, 171, 172, 173, 178, 180, 182, 190, 193, 197, 203, 204, 210, 213, 215, 217, 221, 222, 224, 231, 235, 241, 242, 246, 248, 249, 250, 252, 253, 255, 258, 261, 266, 268, 277, 279, 288, 289, 292, 297, 298, 303, 304, 305, 307, 313, 314, 319, 323, 325, 333, 337, 343, 346, 352, 353, 358, 360, 367, 372, 380, 381, 382, 389, 393, 395, 396, 399, 408, 410, 411, 419, 422, 423, 424, 427, 428, 431, 434, 435, 438, 443, 456, 460, 461, 467, 470, 496, 499, 500, 506, 512, 513, 514, 524, 525, 526, 527, 533, 538, 540, 543, 544, 549, 554, 557, 562, 566, 567, 575, 578, 579, 588, 594, 595, 598, 602, 608

illegally 142, 218

illfitting 269

illuminated 276, 442, 582

illuminates 38, 547

I'm 3, 5, 6, 7, 8, 9, 12, 14, 15, 19, 20, 21, 25, 27, 29, 30, 31, 33, 34, 36, 37, 38, 39, 40, 41, 42, 43, 45, 46, 47, 48, 49, 51, 53, 54, 55, 56, 57, 58, 61, 62, 63, 64, 65, 66, 67, 68, 69, 70, 72, 73, 74, 75, 76, 77, 78, 79, 80, 81, 82, 83, 84, 85, 86, 87, 88, 89, 90, 91, 92, 93, 94, 95, 96, 97, 98, 99, 100, 101, 102, 103, 104, 105, 106, 107, 109, 110, 111, 112, 113, 115, 116, 117, 118, 119, 120, 121, 122, 123, 124, 125, 126, 127, 128, 129, 131, 132, 133, 134, 135, 136, 137, 139, 140, 141, 144, 145, 146, 147, 148, 149, 150, 151, 152, 153, 154, 156, 157, 158, 159, 160, 161, 162, 163, 164, 165, 166, 167, 168, 169, 170, 171, 172, 173, 175, 176, 177, 178, 179, 182, 183, 184, 186, 187, 188, 189, 190, 191, 192, 193, 194, 195, 196, 197, 201, 202, 203, 206, 207, 209, 210, 213, 215, 216, 217, 219, 220, 221, 223, 224, 225, 226, 229, 233, 234, 235, 236, 237, 239, 240, 241, 242, 244, 245, 248, 249, 250, 251, 252, 253, 255, 256, 258, 260, 261, 262, 263, 264, 266, 268, 269, 270, 274, 275, 276, 277, 278, 279, 280, 281, 282, 283, 284, 285, 286, 287, 288, 289, 290, 291, 293, 294, 295, 297, 298, 299, 301, 303, 305, 306, 307, 308, 310, 311, 312, 314, 315, 316, 317, 318, 319, 320, 321, 322, 323, 324, 325, 326, 327, 328, 329, 330, 332, 333, 334, 335, 336, 337, 338, 340, 341, 342, 343, 344, 346, 347, 348, 352, 353, 355, 360, 361, 362, 363, 364, 365, 369, 370, 372, 373, 374, 375, 377, 379, 380, 381, 382, 384, 385, 386, 389, 390, 392, 393, 394, 395, 396, 397, 398, 399, 402, 403, 406, 407, 408, 409, 410, 411, 412, 414, 415, 416, 417, 418, 419, 420, 421, 423, 424, 426, 427, 429, 430, 431, 432, 436, 438, 439, 440, 441, 442, 443, 444, 445, 447, 448, 451, 453, 454, 455, 456, 457, 458, 459, 460, 461, 462, 463, 464, 465, 467, 469, 470, 471, 472, 475, 476, 477, 478, 479, 480, 481, 482, 483, 484, 485, 486, 487, 488, 489, 490, 491, 492, 494, 495, 496, 497, 498, 499, 500, 502, 504, 505, 506, 507, 510, 513, 514, 515, 516, 517, 518, 519, 520, 521, 522, 523, 524, 525, 526, 527, 528, 529, 530, 531, 532, 533, 534, 536, 538, 539, 540, 541, 542, 543, 545, 546, 547, 549, 550, 551, 553, 554, 555, 556, 557, 559, 562, 563, 564, 565, 566, 567, 568, 570, 571, 572, 574, 576, 577, 578, 579, 581, 582, 583, 584, 585, 586, 587, 588, 590, 591, 592, 593, 594, 595, 596, 597, 598, 599, 600, 602, 603, 604, 605, 608

I'm Cinna 35

I'm Finnick 566

images 23, 47, 81, 94, 413, 417, 461, 462, 472, 473, 539, 547, 555, 560, 566, 593

images flood of 405

imagined 50, 116, 133, 212, 227, 409, 496, 544, 609

imagining 29, 70, 76, 311, 369, 438, 553

immensely 573

immigrants	437
immobilized	45, 299
immobilizing	20
impact moment of	516
impales	336
impatiently	367, 372, 383, 422, 518
imperfections	449
implications	246, 423, 509, 530
implying	592
impressed	68, 445, 456
imprinted	410, 498
imprisoned	9, 11, 134, 147, 152, 193, 417, 594
improved	41, 388
improves	140, 485
improving	493
impulses	499
Impulsively	138
impulsiveness	56
inactivity	171
inadvertently	175
incapacitated	131, 390, 429
incarnations	528
inches	55, 65, 94, 176, 177, 184, 192, 305, 309, 316, 349, 355, 361, 364, 427, 431, 477, 534, 551
inching	118, 561
incinerated	403
incineration	402
inciting	3
includes	244, 247, 257, 338, 420, 439, 440, 479, 528, 537, 545
incompleteness	442
incomprehensibly	217
inconvenienced	499
increased	140, 236, 391, 556
increasingly	193, 232
incredibly	176
incriminating	269, 473
indefinitely	93, 274
independently	534
indescribably	220
indicated	397
indicates	329, 445, 514, 529, 560, 567
indicating	79, 231, 275, 278, 369, 389, 413
indifferently	203, 597
indignantly	292
Indirectly	321

indiscriminately 477
individual's 532
induced 409
inducing 474
indulgences 30
indulgently 458
inebriated 243
inexplicably 152, 174, 354, 408, 482, 492, 571
infiltrated 572
infinitely 65
inflamed 100, 135, 140
inflicted 375, 395, 423, 428
information dissemination of 473
information's 475
informers 10
informing 299
infractions 427
infuriates 408
infuses 127
inhabitants 503
inhaled 300
inhales 473
inhaling 4, 205
inheriting 369
inhibited 280
initially 23, 113, 193, 272, 286, 352, 510
initiated 105, 319
initiating 597
injected 78
injects 333
injuries 95, 159, 277, 428, 429, 495
injury risk of 422
innocently 136, 279
innovative 508
inroads 465
ins 575
insectlike 22
insects 101, 102, 343, 347, 379, 386, 391, 392, 393, 400, 453, 454, 456, 459
insects sound of 436
inserts 76, 425
insides 18, 42, 88, 111, 114
insisted 61, 144, 403, 448, 559, 609
insisting 2, 43, 50, 180, 297, 571
insists 27, 75, 138, 313, 328, 345, 367, 515, 536
inspiring 569

installations	267	
installed	188, 201, 478	
installing	503	
instigator	193	
instigators	272	
instinctively	245, 253, 345, 400, 451, 452, 514	
instincts	92, 105, 159, 232, 437	
instructed	79, 318, 463, 495	
instructing	280, 474	
instructs	62, 257, 326, 511, 596	
instruments	442	
insulated	268	
insults	525	
intending	591, 605	
intends	341	
intensely	34, 96, 339, 359, 387	
intentionally	97, 320, 426, 466	
intentions	391, 399	
intently	315, 343, 386, 469	
interacting	459	
intercepts	471	
intercutting	539	
interestingly	22	
interfered	17	
interferes	115, 428	
interlaced	557	
intermingled	204	
intermixed	80	
internal	handful of	508
interpreted	405	
interrupts	191, 248, 411, 430, 447	
intersections	551, 578	
interspersed	123, 580	
intertwines	47	
intervals	473, 475	
intervened	142, 407	
interviewed	219	
interviewer's	414	
interviewing	120	
interviews	61, 63, 66, 67, 102, 128, 162, 185, 191, 193, 299, 327, 332, 373, 439, 465, 496, 549	
interwoven	201, 443	
intestines	302, 478	
intimidated	500	
intones	11	

intrigued 62
introduced 190, 228, 304, 328, 609
introduces 241, 286, 456, 556
introducing 11, 13, 228, 305, 461
intruder 207
invaded 354
invader 117, 544
invasions 532
invented 384, 609
invested 286
invigorating 121
invitations 68, 234
invited 211, 278, 510
invites 35, 477
involuntarily 444
involvement 116
involves 141, 496, 546
irises 566
Ironically 135, 372
irony subtleties of 474
irredeemably 56
irrevocably 468
Isabel 401, 609
ISBN 610
issued 411, 418, 430, 438, 482, 498, 527, 562
issues 293
it| 323, 377
itches 421
it'd 57, 71, 111, 115, 142, 188, 203, 242, 290, 293, 316, 326, 408, 438, 508, 509, 541
items 37, 116, 121, 418
items manufacturing of 282
it'll 85, 135, 177, 224, 320, 434, 471, 487, 489
It's Cinna 161
It's Compartment 425
It's Darius 254
It's Delly 501
It's Effie 332
It's Katniss Everdeen 449
It's Mags 338
It's Primrose Everdeen 12
It's Sunday 59
It's Venia 434
It's|it's 489
I've 8, 15, 19, 20, 22, 23, 25, 30, 31, 33, 34, 35, 39, 40, 41, 44, 48, 49, 52, 53, 55, 56, 57, 61, 62, 63, 66, 69, 70, 72, 75, 79, 80, 81, 82, 83, 85, 86, 87, 88, 89, 90, 91, 92, 93, 94, 95,

99, 100, 102, 103, 106, 107, 108, 110, 111, 112, 117, 121, 122, 123, 125, 126, 127, 128, 129, 130, 131, 132, 134, 135, 136, 138, 139, 140, 141, 146, 147, 148, 149, 150, 153, 154, 155, 156, 157, 159, 161, 162, 166, 167, 169, 172, 175, 176, 179, 182, 184, 185, 188, 189, 192, 193, 195, 196, 197, 199, 200, 201, 202, 203, 205, 206, 212, 214, 216, 217, 218, 219, 220, 222, 225, 226, 231, 233, 234, 235, 240, 242, 243, 244, 245, 248, 252, 253, 260, 262, 263, 264, 265, 266, 271, 273, 275, 276, 277, 278, 281, 284, 290, 291, 292, 295, 302, 303, 305, 308, 309, 310, 314, 319, 320, 322, 324, 331, 333, 338, 339, 342, 343, 349, 352, 354, 357, 360, 361, 363, 365, 366, 369, 372, 374, 382, 384, 385, 388, 393, 396, 406, 416, 421, 422, 426, 429, 436, 437, 438, 439, 440, 446, 449, 450, 454, 456, 460, 463, 475, 476, 477, 480, 481, 482, 485, 486, 487, 490, 491, 495, 498, 499, 504, 505, 506, 507, 510, 515, 517, 519, 520, 522, 523, 526, 527, 528, 530, 537, 539, 540, 541, 543, 552, 553, 554, 557, 562, 564, 569, 571, 573, 574, 577, 579, 580, 586, 587, 591, 596, 601, 603, 608

jabberjay	24, 246, 374, 375, 376, 378
jabberjays	24, 98, 246, 375, 378, 379, 481, 493, 531, 565
jabberjay's	374
Jabberjays	375
jabs	184, 526
jacker	99, 101, 102, 104, 105, 106, 109, 110, 113, 114, 132, 134, 135, 136, 173, 192, 275, 496, 498, 512, 547, 560
jackers	98, 99, 101, 102, 104, 106, 112, 115, 123, 174, 523, 551, 565, 593
jackets	179, 608
jacket's	77, 96, 253
Jackson	537, 540, 541, 542, 543, 544, 547, 549, 550, 552, 553, 556, 557, 558, 559, 561, 562, 563, 564, 571, 572
Jackson's	547
Jacky Harper	608
James Proimos	1, 609
jams	151, 531
Jane Collins	609
January	15, 59
jarred	350
jarring	207
jars	471
Jason Dravis	608
jellies	304
Jen Rees	608
jeopardized	572
jerked	177
jerks	44, 119, 370, 568, 589
Jess White	608
jets	47
jeweled	68, 283
jewels	37, 65, 146, 176, 306
jimmies	551
JJ	378

Joanie 609
jobs 313, 431, 503
job's 85, 115
jogging 80, 525
jogs 455
Johanna 309, 311, 332, 362, 363, 365, 366, 367, 368, 369, 370, 371, 372, 373, 375, 377, 378, 379, 382, 383, 384, 385, 386, 387, 388, 389, 390, 391, 394, 396, 398, 399, 414, 423, 432, 434, 517, 518, 521, 525, 526, 527, 528, 529, 530, 531, 532, 535, 536, 579, 596, 597
Johanna Mason 23, 296, 309, 315, 317, 327, 328, 363, 369, 373, 395, 402, 413, 481, 494, 516
Johannas 492
Johanna's 317, 363, 367, 369, 376, 379, 390, 525, 526, 527, 529, 532, 535, 541
John Mason 608
joined 68, 340, 365, 383, 551, 564
joining 41, 317, 605
joins 54, 386, 508, 519, 534, 537, 567, 607
joints 89, 104, 106, 143, 199
jokes 67, 144, 191, 317, 319, 329, 602
joke's 292
joking 28, 107, 194, 310, 381, 430, 489, 500, 507, 597
jolted 571
jolts 111
Joy Simpkins 608
judges 58, 279
judging 26, 30, 371, 385
juices 52, 88, 263
jumped 49, 59, 211, 339
jumping 277, 352, 482, 533, 600
jumps 38, 57, 168, 205, 361, 472
jumpsuit 304, 333, 334, 339, 354, 355, 356, 364, 365, 366
jumpsuits 36, 352, 362, 445
jungle| 373
jungle|green 413
jungle's 384, 391
just| 316
just|couldn't 195
just|I 57, 60, 422
just|if 163
just|Peeta 419
just|the 328
just|those 377
Justice Building 10, 19, 22, 23, 28, 29, 40, 59, 228, 231, 232, 235, 244, 254, 265, 272, 273, 282, 294, 327, 330, 402, 405, 486, 503, 510, 513, 514
jutted 486
Karyn Browne 608

Kate Egan 608

Kathleen Donohoe 608

Kathy 609

katniss 4, 7, 13, 20, 21, 22, 28, 29, 35, 36, 37, 38, 39, 40, 42, 48, 49, 54, 59, 60, 62, 63, 68, 69, 70, 72, 74, 75, 76, 78, 94, 110, 112, 123, 127, 128, 131, 135, 136, 137, 140, 145, 154, 157, 158, 163, 167, 168, 169, 170, 172, 175, 176, 177, 180, 182, 194, 195, 197, 206, 214, 215, 216, 220, 221, 225, 231, 233, 234, 235, 240, 241, 242, 250, 251, 252, 253, 258, 261, 264, 265, 267, 270, 283, 292, 293, 295, 297, 304, 305, 309, 311, 321, 322, 326, 328, 329, 333, 338, 340, 342, 360, 372, 373, 374, 375, 376, 377, 379, 380, 381, 384, 385, 387, 389, 391, 393, 394, 397, 398, 399, 400, 403, 413, 414, 418, 419, 423, 424, 425, 430, 432, 434, 435, 436, 443, 445, 446, 449, 451, 452, 454, 456, 459, 462, 464, 466, 471, 474, 475, 477, 480, 481, 484, 487, 488, 489, 495, 496, 497, 498, 499, 500, 501, 502, 504, 506, 511, 512, 513, 514, 518, 519, 523, 524, 530, 536, 537, 540, 550, 553, 556, 557, 561, 562, 563, 565, 566, 570, 571, 572, 574, 575, 579, 581, 586, 594, 596, 597, 602

Katniss Everdeen 10, 13, 68, 182, 196, 209, 286, 402, 403, 412, 421, 441, 449, 457, 473, 514, 547, 556, 587, 588, 599

Katniss Everdeen's 71

Katniss|he's 417

Katniss|how 473

Katniss's 232, 238, 295, 330, 371, 372, 377, 438, 441, 459, 496, 575, 605

keepers 308

keeping job of 343

keepsakes 527

kernels 118

keys 428

kicked 606

kicking 119, 191, 205, 599

kicks 222, 232, 309, 358, 440, 548, 566, 583

kidnapped 429, 594

kids 5, 6, 10, 11, 12, 15, 17, 20, 25, 46, 51, 112, 155, 162, 165, 201, 204, 211, 227, 249, 250, 255, 259, 266, 267, 286, 287, 297, 299, 311, 317, 348, 381, 405, 420, 437, 500, 509, 518, 553, 609

Kill Peeta 548, 549

KILL SNOW 421

killed 15, 59, 76, 84, 109, 113, 119, 128, 129, 132, 152, 168, 169, 170, 200, 201, 207, 233, 237, 247, 250, 253, 256, 262, 270, 286, 288, 294, 299, 300, 301, 302, 314, 318, 320, 324, 333, 367, 377, 390, 397, 403, 405, 407, 412, 417, 442, 481, 485, 495, 502, 509, 515, 539, 544, 572, 587, 590, 592, 594, 596, 597

killed| 199

killed|do 177

killers 81, 313

Killing Brutus 413

killing aftermath of 438

killing dangers of 510

killings 274

kills 106, 129, 155, 167, 394, 451, 462, 491, 499, 514, 525, 545, 563

kinder 397, 460, 528, 554

kindest 557

kindled 607

kinds 21, 27, 206, 260, 303, 444, 507

kissed 138, 211, 212, 236, 293, 365, 380, 441, 471, 506, 575

kisses 38, 39, 73, 78, 139, 140, 182, 189, 192, 195, 212, 219, 239, 275, 292, 295, 308, 334, 380, 381, 469, 494, 504, 506, 507, 530, 594

kissing 138, 148, 190, 229, 245, 264, 276, 309, 341, 382, 494, 506, 524, 530, 532, 605

Kitchen Duties 410

kits 585

kneaded 284

kneeling 516

kneels 153, 580

knees 2, 17, 36, 92, 103, 104, 118, 120, 124, 137, 150, 182, 188, 189, 231, 253, 272, 287, 290, 311, 334, 336, 342, 352, 354, 355, 362, 375, 390, 393, 450, 514, 515, 520, 581, 591, 599, 600

knickknacks 433, 579

knobs 426

knocked 12, 142, 185, 254, 278, 334, 367, 398, 473, 478, 488, 495, 531

knockers 583

knocking 30, 31, 56, 61, 150, 189, 220, 223, 284, 397, 458, 581, 593

knockoff 242

knocks 14, 118, 233, 295, 311, 370

knots 41, 52, 186, 255, 291, 314, 325, 432, 484, 492, 493, 542

know| 430

know|I 210

know|things 246

knowledge|real 545

knuckles 3

labeled 563

labs 100, 436

laced 219, 337, 497, 534, 573

laces 352, 568, 604

lacked 60

lacks 294

ladders 183, 453

Ladies 12, 78, 182, 299, 334, 534

ladles 291

lake's 216

Lamb Stew 555

lamely 593

lamps 482

land   circle of 370

landscapes 74

lapdogs 86, 576

lapels 239

lapping 365

laps 354

largest 296

lashed 256

lashes 31, 65, 175, 255, 256, 342, 435

lasted 81

lasts 37, 67, 77, 473

latches 438, 558

Latecomers 10

laterally 444, 557

lathered 565

Latin 519

latter's 61

laughed 56, 189

laughs 26, 45, 53, 67, 68, 133, 167, 178, 214, 227, 240, 265, 307, 323, 344, 452, 520, 524, 558, 593

laugh's 120

launched 73, 93, 445, 457, 512, 553

launchers 93, 437, 503

launches 116, 217, 548

launching 602

launchpad 510

Lavinia 545, 560

lawns 287

laws 10, 202, 286, 609

layering 480

layers 33, 331, 359, 424, 568, 570, 576

laying 389

lays 196, 263, 358, 368, 415, 583

lazily 101

leached 199

leaches 366

leaching 107, 354

leaders 406, 410, 503, 598

leads 73, 77, 105, 114, 132, 155, 186, 189, 197, 221, 226, 231, 232, 240, 246, 301, 303, 451, 492, 512, 529, 531, 552, 553, 559, 587

leaked 405

leaking 30

leaned 17

leans 9, 21, 43, 48, 78, 160, 182, 305, 319, 323, 412, 426, 460, 506, 518

leaping 101, 325, 391, 582

leaps 176, 495

learner 336

leaves   canopy of   127
leaves   rustle of   468
lectures   531
ledgers   232
Leeg   537, 542, 547, 548, 550, 552, 553, 555, 556, 558, 559, 562, 564, 571
Leevy   255, 435, 440, 441
leftovers   88, 388
leg|what   135
leggings   569, 574
legs   2, 33, 67, 78, 90, 175, 176, 181, 185, 223, 255, 352, 357, 380, 392, 396, 443, 444, 483, 546, 607
leg's   167
lemony   47
lends   346
lengths   208, 251, 450, 588
length's   534
lenses   550
Leslie Garych   608
lessened   126
lessens   177
lessons   52, 64, 319
letting   64, 69, 106, 113, 123, 163, 180, 183, 208, 214, 215, 269, 308, 309, 349, 370, 430, 557, 584, 601
Level Five   474
Level Seven   426
levels   425, 439, 444, 445, 478, 485, 498, 522
levers   559
licked   144, 596
licks   166, 350
lids   477
lies   24, 44, 78, 79, 114, 131, 135, 137, 162, 165, 175, 246, 260, 288, 341, 354, 355, 358, 373, 393, 396, 418, 419, 434, 438, 444, 448, 463, 469, 479, 486, 501, 534, 551, 560, 563, 582, 593
lies   mess of   560
life   loss of   549
lifetimes   289
lifted   13, 17, 76, 87, 103, 116, 169, 248, 376, 404, 408, 411, 418, 433
lifting   46, 190, 254, 451, 458
lifts   91, 216, 254, 355, 358, 359, 363, 376, 391, 427, 445, 447, 536, 601
lighted   38
lightened   59, 149
lightens   54
like| 573
like|sunset   225
liked   24, 59, 66, 124, 212, 296, 310, 434

likens   521
likes   46, 161, 199, 202, 244, 338, 359, 431, 478, 500, 518
lilies   91
limbed   564
limbless   447
limbs   92, 97, 102, 104, 177, 181, 199, 339, 356, 357, 374, 438, 449, 546, 565, 584, 586
limitations   440
limits   590
limping   86, 345
limply   413
limps   181, 269
lined   37, 66, 73, 104, 151, 227, 245, 426, 569
lingered   212
lingering   149
lingers   74, 208, 442, 604
lips   7, 14, 16, 25, 34, 64, 65, 67, 68, 69, 71, 78, 82, 88, 125, 126, 133, 137, 138, 139,
140, 151, 152, 154, 158, 160, 176, 178, 181, 182, 183, 184, 188, 207, 212, 213, 223, 225, 229,
230, 231, 235, 237, 238, 252, 257, 259, 271, 294, 298, 300, 304, 306, 307, 312, 331, 341, 344,
353, 375, 376, 380, 418, 424, 435, 446, 452, 457, 471, 477, 480, 487, 495, 506, 507, 515, 521,
526, 548, 555, 561, 566, 567, 583, 585, 598, 605, 607
liquids   183
liquor   odors of   204
listened   8, 552
listening   15, 20, 111, 146, 174, 179, 182, 194, 217, 275, 429, 454, 491, 495, 512
listens   343
littered   116, 417, 585
Little Rue   460
littler   59
live   proximity of 386
lived   28, 104, 144, 155, 161, 250, 405, 406, 496, 554, 599, 602
lizards   346
Lizette Serrano   608
ll   118, 125, 131, 178
lobs   302
located   141
locating   542
locations   272
lockdown   272, 474, 475, 481
locked   15, 45, 75, 104, 106, 118, 127, 173, 182, 193, 207, 261, 275, 279, 280, 281, 339,
352, 414, 417, 422, 459
locking   295, 311, 573, 604
locks   34, 254, 460, 566, 577, 595
lodges   31, 80
Logically   515
logs   200

lonelier	127, 148
loneliness	29
longingly	72, 107, 161
longtime	608
lookalike	43
looked	6, 17, 42, 53, 143, 194, 211, 226, 233, 262, 322, 361, 391, 501, 523, 525, 578
looking	4, 6, 11, 13, 15, 25, 32, 42, 47, 51, 57, 67, 73, 74, 79, 84, 89, 119, 122, 125, 126, 132, 141, 143, 151, 159, 160, 174, 183, 185, 188, 191, 194, 212, 216, 220, 224, 237, 242, 246, 261, 282, 289, 291, 310, 311, 315, 320, 322, 324, 329, 346, 361, 369, 390, 400, 403, 409, 426, 431, 433, 435, 438, 440, 452, 461, 465, 487, 494, 503, 507, 511, 515, 527, 532, 548, 549, 550, 556, 564, 567, 576, 577, 580, 581, 584, 588, 589, 590, 591, 599, 606
looks	2, 11, 19, 30, 34, 35, 39, 41, 42, 44, 45, 53, 66, 67, 74, 98, 106, 108, 115, 120, 134, 135, 136, 140, 142, 155, 157, 171, 172, 183, 190, 203, 205, 206, 218, 219, 222, 234, 235, 240, 241, 258, 260, 269, 278, 281, 285, 296, 298, 299, 300, 304, 308, 310, 314, 315, 320, 322, 326, 330, 346, 356, 359, 361, 369, 375, 380, 384, 385, 397, 407, 409, 410, 411, 412, 414, 421, 422, 431, 432, 434, 435, 439, 440, 441, 443, 444, 446, 447, 452, 458, 461, 462, 465, 484, 496, 500, 524, 526, 529, 534, 537, 539, 542, 545, 547, 554, 556, 568, 569, 570, 578, 587, 589, 594, 596, 597, 604
looms	603
loops	3, 255, 363, 389
loosely	166, 392, 427
loses	71, 93, 152, 178, 364, 382, 478, 522
losing grief of	500
losing idea of	195, 211
losing verge of	470
losses	229, 572, 607
louder	60, 180, 386, 521
loudly	205, 343, 498, 562
love|I	72
lovebirds pair of	206
loved	5, 19, 28, 29, 72, 184, 193, 260, 262, 295, 359, 413, 448, 489, 491, 523, 535, 543, 585, 597
loved voices of	481
Lover Boy	86, 105, 115, 151
lovers	72, 130, 138, 202, 245, 297, 308, 328, 378, 486, 491
lovers|Peeta	130
loves	112, 182, 378, 407, 487, 490, 497, 498, 519, 520, 575
lowered	142
lowers	153, 270, 448
lowest	56
lugging	59
lullabies	98
lulled	293, 365
lulling	158
lumps	102, 114, 134, 416

lunatics 232
lunched 85
lunges 25, 357
lungfuls 531
lunging 564
lungs 12, 74, 92, 146, 151, 341, 565, 586
lurches 221, 227
lured 87
luring 39, 258, 499
lurking 262
lush|she's 67
luxuriously 350
luxury lap of 590
Lyme 507, 508, 509, 515
Lyme's 508, 509
lyrics 468, 600
maces 22, 337
machine row of 452
machines 396, 495, 559, 560, 607
Madge 7, 8, 21, 148, 196, 218, 219, 244, 245, 246, 258, 259, 293, 299, 316, 349, 376, 377, 405, 605
Madge's 7, 8, 10, 23, 108, 245, 295, 299
maggots 241
magnified 71, 582
Mags 318, 319, 338, 339, 341, 343, 344, 345, 346, 347, 348, 349, 350, 351, 352, 353, 356, 360, 361, 364, 365, 372, 377, 378, 441, 460, 529, 566
Mags's 339, 345, 350, 353
maimed 43, 405
maintaining 405, 465, 596
makeover 222, 435
makes 4, 6, 14, 20, 25, 26, 29, 33, 37, 42, 47, 48, 57, 58, 62, 65, 67, 72, 76, 82, 84, 94, 97, 101, 102, 103, 105, 109, 111, 119, 121, 122, 126, 130, 131, 134, 135, 140, 146, 148, 149, 154, 158, 160, 163, 164, 165, 167, 176, 178, 180, 181, 184, 185, 186, 191, 192, 196, 199, 207, 218, 219, 220, 222, 226, 227, 232, 237, 239, 241, 244, 252, 259, 269, 270, 275, 278, 279, 280, 281, 283, 287, 290, 291, 296, 300, 302, 304, 312, 313, 314, 315, 317, 320, 325, 329, 333, 338, 343, 344, 348, 351, 353, 354, 356, 359, 360, 373, 379, 388, 391, 411, 413, 421, 427, 435, 436, 444, 445, 447, 448, 465, 466, 479, 482, 488, 495, 497, 501, 506, 507, 517, 522, 527, 530, 535, 536, 541, 542, 545, 548, 549, 550, 551, 553, 574, 579, 590, 594, 600, 602, 603, 604, 606
makeup layers of 284
makeup streaks of 443
malfunctioned 224
manacles 531, 539, 589
managed 28, 80, 90, 117, 130, 131, 201, 212, 273, 296, 361, 404, 410, 416, 427, 434, 457, 478, 572
manages 11, 226, 237, 260, 274, 284, 337, 493, 515, 558

maneuvering	368
mangled	183
maniacally	4
manicured	568
manipulated	381, 441
manipulates	479
manipulating	250, 314, 586, 591
Manipulative	524
mannequins	568
manner's	412, 454
manning	389, 511, 570
man's	24, 95, 185, 234, 254, 277, 278, 512
mansion's	573
manually	548, 576
manufactured	137, 444
manufactures	445
mapped	229
maps	411, 442
marched	144, 294
marches	19
marching	267, 581
market's	6
marks	15, 92, 96, 144, 248, 414, 470, 514, 538, 596, 599, 606
marred	360
marrying	212
Mary Beth Bass	609
mashed	2, 25, 58, 304, 420
masks	37, 245, 272, 312, 531, 550, 559, 563
massaged	223
massages	217, 424, 495
massaging	41
mastered	52, 126
masterminded	428
masters	472
matched	2, 310
matches	82, 109, 113, 226, 270, 305, 315, 475, 544
matching	9, 36, 55, 219, 278, 312
mated	24, 246, 374
materialized	59, 426, 471, 605
materializes	87, 126, 183, 395, 408, 584
Materializing	358
material's	443
mates	575
mats	320, 346, 347
mattered	12, 57, 63, 298, 413, 454

matters	328, 365, 435, 530, 540, 581, 594
mauled	143
Maybe Finnick	390
Maybe Haymitch	297
Maybe Haymitch's	126
Maybe I'd	330
Maybe I'll	136, 471, 523
Maybe I'm	154, 182, 399, 481
Maybe Johanna	391
Maybe|because	195
Mayor Undersee	10
Mayor Undersee's	244, 246, 299
mayor|	605
mayor's	7, 108, 218, 228, 244, 245, 247, 250, 405, 605
Maysilee	299, 301, 302
Maysilee Donner	287, 299, 300, 301
Maysilee Donner's	369
me|	252, 405
me|but	324
me|my	491
me|no	161, 497
me|what	289
me|you'd	116
meadows	112
Meadow's	143, 605
meals	53, 54, 404, 406, 410, 435, 482, 587
meal's	25, 295
mean|go	578
mean|I	419
mean|some	445
meandering	312
Meaning Peeta	406
measurements	386
Meat Grinder	563, 564, 572
meat chunk of	347
meat smell of	120
meats	346
medical box of	478
medicated	498
medications	600
medicine tube of	367
medicines	114, 203, 587, 594, 607
medicine's	137
medics	447, 455, 539, 547, 585, 591, 599
Meet Effie	50

meeting/war 411
meetings 242, 504
meeting's 534
meets 342, 466, 583
Mellark's 479
melodies 24, 174, 247
meltdown 437, 513
melted 99, 304, 405, 571, 587
melting 470
melts 42, 266, 271, 458, 563
memorials 607
memories 95, 104, 142, 177, 180, 402, 408, 466, 467, 496, 497, 498, 500, 501, 505, 530, 536, 540, 560, 602
menacing 60, 175
mentioned 42, 46, 114, 147, 217, 299, 372, 414
mentioning 50, 481
mentions 107, 267, 463, 544
mentoring 288
mentors 71, 162, 207, 217, 221, 296, 305, 318, 348, 350
mentor's 51, 69
merchants 16, 49, 201, 299
mercifully 23
merrily 220
mesmerized 17, 174, 359
mesmerizing 308
messages 112, 348, 411
Messalla 447, 450, 456, 461, 545, 546, 547, 548, 550, 554, 555, 558, 562, 563, 571
Messalla sight of 453
Messalla's 459
messed 527
messing 7, 54, 146, 369, 386, 499
metal lump of 470
metal piece of 349
metal sound of 178
methodically 346
methods 107
Meticulously 471
Michael Collins 198, 609
microphones 232
midafternoon 346
midair 436
midcalf 355
midmorning 360
might've 311
migrating 505

mike's 513
mildew odors of 228
mildly 383
miles 23, 90, 93, 158, 249, 300, 371, 396, 405, 436, 493, 507
militaristic 416
militarized 536
Military Tactics 530
milking 47
mimicked 481
mimicking 115, 168
mimics 4, 265, 289
minced 463
mind|hm 195
mindlessly 374
minds 25, 85, 132, 146, 319, 329, 354, 545, 579
mind's 172, 592
mine|but 225
mined 23, 116, 550, 558
miners 3, 23, 95, 200, 251, 255, 267, 273, 299, 402, 503, 511, 515
miner's 36, 400
Miners 454
mines 5, 6, 13, 16, 32, 78, 99, 116, 117, 118, 119, 120, 135, 143, 200, 201, 211, 226, 251, 262, 266, 267, 268, 273, 284, 294, 369, 402, 403, 404, 479, 503, 557, 607
minesweeping 547
mingled 371
minted 533
minute's 92
mirrored 473, 551, 555
mirrors 361
miscalculated 389
mischievously 59, 157
misdirected 8
miseries 223
misery look of 553
misgivings 110
mishaps 470
misjudged 33, 90, 152, 483
mislabeled 539
misled 192
Miss Everdeen 204, 206, 208, 210, 277, 321, 591, 598
missed 32, 79, 163, 383, 457, 530, 541, 580
misses 80, 422, 453
missiles 410, 444, 471, 474, 481, 486, 503, 538
missions 531
mist droplets of 351

mistaking 374

mistreatment 428

mistreats 90

misusing 530

Mitchell 537, 538, 547, 548, 549, 551, 552, 553, 571, 572, 577

Mitchell's 546, 547, 548

mixing 359

moaning 98, 152, 179, 331, 580

moans 179, 355, 392, 514

mocked 319

mocking 76, 212, 266

mockingbirds 24, 246

mockingjay 1, 24, 30, 77, 112, 113, 114, 123, 126, 133, 174, 181, 196, 219, 228, 230, 239, 242, 243, 244, 246, 247, 269, 273, 275, 282, 285, 295, 299, 320, 329, 334, 335, 343, 356, 367, 374, 380, 395, 398, 400, 406, 407, 411, 418, 419, 420, 422, 423, 424, 425, 429, 432, 433, 434, 439, 440, 448, 450, 457, 459, 460, 463, 467, 468, 471, 478, 481, 484, 485, 487, 488, 495, 502, 510, 515, 517, 521, 524, 532, 533, 534, 536, 537, 539, 549, 554, 555, 556, 562, 572, 587, 588, 591, 593, 595, 597, 599, 600, 601, 609

Mockingjay Deal 596

Mockingjay DEDICATION CONTENTS 610

Mockingjay|could 407

mockingjays 24, 112, 113, 125, 127, 174, 230, 246, 467, 469, 505, 600, 608

mockingjay's 123, 282

Mockingjays 246, 274, 531, 560

Mockingjay's 553

models 23

moisturized 47

molded 2

mollified 460

moments 21, 26, 74, 104, 150, 164, 165, 173, 180, 205, 243, 246, 256, 259, 329, 341, 365, 381, 386, 387, 432, 437, 441, 459, 470, 495, 528, 532, 545, 558, 568, 580, 601, 607

moment's 140, 177, 356

Moments 351

Mon 354

money security of 293

monitored 184

monitoring 193, 235

monitors 396

monkeys 354, 356, 357, 358, 359, 365, 366, 370, 375, 562, 565

monkey's 358, 372

monsters 413, 564, 601

monstrosities 562

months 7, 15, 28, 29, 59, 60, 105, 196, 199, 216, 220, 221, 263, 272, 282, 286, 291, 302, 315, 330, 430, 440, 492, 507, 524, 534, 568, 603

moods 62

moonlight patches of 288

moons 390

mopping 587

mops 493

more|sophisticated 188

morning's 37, 388, 447

morphling 259, 308, 348, 358, 359, 372, 378, 412, 471, 505, 516, 517, 518, 526, 527, 535, 547, 586, 587, 593, 600, 601

morphling twilight of 516

morphlings 315, 319, 320, 331

morphling's 359

morphs 543

mortifying 524

motes 605

mothers 5

mother's 2, 5, 16, 17, 20, 23, 77, 138, 143, 154, 206, 214, 249, 259, 263, 279, 281, 291, 299, 315, 450, 455, 482, 498, 586, 602, 603

motions 19, 106, 127, 359, 418, 606

motivated 110, 115, 323, 557, 575, 588, 600

motivational 525

motives 61, 392, 454

mountains 5, 32, 502, 506, 545

mountainsides 508, 510

mounted 232

mounts 25

mouthing 583

mouths 5, 6, 136, 183, 350, 370, 376, 435, 469, 470, 518, 564, 565, 568, 582, 583

move|is 553

moved 15, 20, 28, 45, 133, 159, 194, 195, 273, 320, 321, 342, 352, 356, 365, 372, 396, 410, 422, 431, 441, 511, 531

movements 89, 232, 366, 411, 430, 435

moves 21, 40, 122, 125, 158, 171, 178, 358, 375, 421, 425, 426, 461, 462, 480, 482, 491, 495, 581, 608

mows 580

mud layer of 135

muddled 181, 513

muddling 353

mudslides 503

muffled 523, 542

muffles 82

muffling 427

mugs 298

mulling 115, 581

mulls 474

multidirectional 484

multilevel	559
multiplied	447
mumbles	54, 344, 364
murdered	177, 299, 303, 410, 467, 553
murderer	468, 469
murderer's	468
murdering	109
murders	248, 497
murmuring	12, 71, 363, 379
murmurs	85, 229, 435, 529, 567, 578
muscled	21, 507
muscles	4, 12, 32, 62, 70, 84, 87, 94, 119, 178, 183, 199, 288, 293, 336, 376, 473, 483, 530, 566, 586
musically	321
musicians	235, 239
music's	240
mussing	414
must've	217, 256, 356, 584
muted	215, 225, 489, 588
mutely	312, 585
mutilated	257, 270, 313, 549
mutilation	262, 569
muttation	261, 374, 539
muttation pack of	284
muttations	24, 98, 175, 226, 246, 261, 351, 362, 467
muttering	30, 545
mutters	137, 259, 446, 515, 528
mutts	24, 175, 176, 177, 178, 179, 180, 181, 183, 192, 195, 226, 261, 357, 512, 531, 534, 541, 561, 562, 564, 565, 566, 572, 574, 588, 596, 597, 607
mutual glue of	470
Mutually	259
my/Cinna's	219
mysteriously	489
mystified	70
Nah	265
nails	3, 33, 50, 64, 74, 78, 119, 176, 183, 184, 187, 188, 216, 217, 325, 433, 434, 456, 594, 605
Nakedness	135
named	2, 28, 34, 51, 142, 203, 215, 255, 377, 405, 446, 447, 507, 537, 569, 604
names	4, 5, 10, 11, 12, 14, 25, 27, 38, 97, 165, 237, 239, 296, 299, 346, 456, 486, 491
name's	54, 70, 269, 289, 532
naming	432
napped	571
naps	387, 602
narrowed	574

narrowing   process of   286
nation's   445, 555
natives   498
natural| 351
natured   165, 191, 286, 488
naturedly   69, 221, 241
navigating   167, 335
nearer   153
nearest   212, 275, 368, 556
nearing   77, 275, 514
nears   501
neatly   80, 96, 114, 116, 123, 127, 311, 420, 518, 527
necklaces   468, 469
necks   564, 568
nectar   drop of   104
needles   120, 121, 123, 137, 167, 270, 361, 536
Needling   110
needn't   314
negativity   457
neglected   177, 229, 562
Negotiating   572
negotiations 340
neighbors   15, 273, 286, 515
Neither Peeta   391
nervously   45
nervousness   50, 78
nested   215
nestled   84
nests   28, 97, 99, 107, 113, 114, 192, 265, 275, 458, 514, 570
nets   6, 28, 115, 314, 325, 392, 544
netted   549
nettles   259
neutrally   217, 509
newcomers   35, 362
newfound   325, 507
newscaster   282
newspapers   293
next| 330
next|you're   249
nicer   5, 21
Nick Martin   608
nicknamed   3, 139, 317, 367, 503
nickname's   317
night   dark of   442
night|to   413

night|well   413
nightgowns   29, 431, 576
nightlock   169, 446, 539, 554, 566, 577, 578, 583, 599
nightmares   226, 236, 243, 244, 280, 288, 297, 312, 313, 324, 418, 463, 481, 484, 504, 566, 579, 593, 605, 607, 608
nightmares   stuff of   217
nightmarish   103, 496
nights   6, 77, 109, 157, 158, 161, 324, 530
night's   48, 101, 292, 324
Nine Oh Eight   425, 426
nodding   31, 55, 69, 270, 362, 491, 534
nods   10, 20, 21, 38, 46, 47, 48, 101, 109, 112, 202, 209, 248, 263, 271, 290, 301, 325, 331, 337, 355, 367, 368, 382, 409, 413, 435, 441, 445, 457, 459, 497, 533, 543, 565, 572, 579
noiselessly   84, 185
none's   197
nonexistent   218, 396
nonissue   422
nonsensical   359
nonthreatening   543
noodles   42, 122
normal   sheath of   439
North America   10
nosedive   461
noses   562, 568, 582
nostrils   341, 351, 546
Note Giver   608
notepad   441
notes   24, 53, 126, 174, 243, 293, 297, 421, 425, 426, 450, 467, 600
notes   handful of   123
nothing|shiny   545
nothingness   wall of   121
Nothing's   140, 163
noticeably   556
noticed   17, 28, 39, 48, 50, 68, 113, 126, 161, 253, 268, 305, 425
notices   26, 267, 411, 469, 539, 558
noticing   75, 137, 444, 459
notified   479, 544
noting   539
novels   608, 609
November   149
now| 149, 553
Now's   175, 420, 550
Nuclear History   421
nuclear   threat of   519
nudges   51, 163, 201, 363

nudging	161, 344, 518
nuked	444
nukes	416, 433
number|it's	176
numbered	356
numbly	397, 403, 502, 571, 584
numbness	15
numbs	263
nursing	192, 224, 266, 498
Nut's	509, 513
NY	609
obediently	128, 135, 139, 174, 367, 455, 484
obeyed	428
objections	326, 534, 550, 574
Objectively	192
objects	57, 207, 278, 337, 367, 559
obligated	289
obliged	574
obliterated	10, 248, 373, 402, 409
obliterating	510
obscenities	30, 258
obscured	304, 311, 339, 408, 429, 476
observed	206
observes	522
observing	46
obsessed	379
obsessions	326
obsessively	78, 484
obstacles	173
obviously	22, 50, 61, 84, 86, 117, 184, 215, 218, 233, 248, 275, 290, 310, 312, 313, 328, 335, 400, 425, 460, 462, 468, 475, 484, 496, 578
Obviously Haymitch	26
Obviously I'm	155
Obviously I've	391
occasions	4, 16
occupied	161, 269, 357, 358, 378, 383, 408, 524, 576
occupies	248, 552
occupying	499
occurred	14, 187, 232, 594
occurs	108, 394, 423
Octavia	34, 186, 187, 190, 216, 217, 223, 240, 282, 283, 303, 315, 325, 427, 431, 432, 433, 434, 435, 441, 520, 594, 595
Octavia's	65, 427, 434, 435, 594
October	59
Odair	444

oddly	32, 34, 99, 335
of|	14
of|being	195
of|of	98
offended	496
offender	326
offenses	267
offered	144, 218, 259, 297, 307, 308, 464, 505, 526, 574
offers	9, 41, 92, 97, 164, 183, 209, 225, 246, 253, 347, 349, 350, 365, 430, 488, 567, 576
offices	587
officially	23, 201, 225, 233, 244, 266, 293, 330, 457, 488, 490, 521, 530
officials	3, 5, 9, 108, 142, 193, 207, 406, 598
offs	367
offshoots	559
Ohhh	107
oiled	429, 433, 514
oiling	315, 317
oils	41
olds	10, 525
on|	417, 604
one|	194
one|could	501
One|two|three|on	81
ones	10, 13, 19, 51, 52, 58, 62, 66, 67, 77, 85, 99, 105, 106, 107, 112, 126, 131, 150, 156, 170, 177, 184, 216, 219, 227, 236, 251, 262, 286, 288, 290, 295, 303, 370, 377, 398, 419, 426, 439, 448, 453, 456, 467, 494, 497, 526, 531, 533, 535, 557, 563, 584, 585, 586
one's	7, 61, 158, 216, 321, 346, 355, 459, 463, 466, 475, 520, 563
onions	27, 35, 528
online	609
onlookers	458
Only|I	75
Only|no	75
ooh	69, 278
oozes	102
oozing	135, 364, 494
openings	115, 358
openly	61, 64, 279, 383, 406, 544
operated	172
operates	6, 483
operating	131, 235
opiates	260
opinions	144, 309, 601
opponents	105, 163, 172, 293, 301, 306
opportunities	286, 441

opposed 190, 366

opposing 576

opposing idea of 332

oppressors 556

options 41, 89, 107, 115, 368, 461, 597

Or|already 189

or|is 128

Or|or| 157

oranges 35, 211, 212

orchards 107, 227, 231

orchestrated 189, 376

orders| 549

organized 262, 402, 404, 417

organizing 223

organs 443

orifices 582

originated 397

other's 50, 61, 98, 130, 165, 183, 237, 244, 259, 310, 315, 361, 430, 470, 521, 529, 595

Otherwise I'd 288

out| 246

out|and 529

Outbursts 490

outcropping 92

outerwear 579

outfits 36, 199, 219, 223, 273, 299, 308, 447, 476, 567

outfoxed 169

outgrew 306

outgrown 430

outgun 533

outlasted 247

outlaws 284

outlived 569, 591

outnumbered 383

outperforming 61

outscored 171

outshone 39

outside| 425

outsmarted 162, 207

outsmarting 129, 189

outweighed 474, 503

ovals 184

ovens 17, 21

over| 587

overcame 100

overcomes 284, 290

overcook	129
overcooking	329
overestimated	233
overflowing	164
overheard	87, 221
Overlander	609
overlapped	500
overlooked	267, 284, 492, 540
overlooking	4, 469
overlooks	41, 567
overpowered	178
overreacting	409, 535
overrides	429
overrode	455
overseeing	40
overshot	116
oversized	207, 411
overtaking	228
overthinking	532
overthrown	444
overtook	607
overwhelmed	81, 152, 272, 299
owed	153, 296, 360
owes	499
owned	287, 405
Owning	143
owns	218
oysters	387, 388
paces	392, 482
pacing	199, 477, 508
pack(s)	476
packages	211
packed	39, 67, 79, 118, 153, 166, 211, 229, 245, 264, 445, 538, 577, 584
packs	3, 79, 93, 126, 127, 150, 172, 179, 300, 301, 476, 538, 558
pacts	301
padded	279, 333, 395, 396, 497
paddling	215, 338
pages	27, 297, 424, 607
pain howls of	178
painfully	181, 182, 261, 553
painkillers	257, 570
pain's	518
painstakingly	583
painted	32, 37, 52, 133, 217, 226, 322, 407, 412, 433, 447, 449, 476, 485, 546, 588

paintings 225, 226, 309

paints 359

pales 262

pallets 448

palms 58, 68, 71, 72, 101, 375, 408, 415, 449, 457, 522, 581

pampered handful of 410

paneled 24

panels 31, 75, 411

Panem 4, 8, 10, 25, 32, 56, 66, 67, 71, 118, 142, 157, 158, 165, 191, 209, 210, 235, 237, 245, 271, 299, 305, 331, 397, 403, 413, 425, 439, 440, 458, 462, 466, 472, 481, 515, 516, 519, 521, 532, 556, 568, 587, 588

Panem anthem of 19

Panem history of 10, 23

Panem joke of 189

Panem laughingstock of 11

Panem oppression of 596

Panem rest of 147

Panem seal of 265, 555

Panem's 465

Panem's assassin of 598

panicked 149, 253, 366, 510, 535, 576

panting 81, 88, 137, 175, 287, 341, 342, 357, 358, 370, 566, 583

paper slip of 12

paper square of 299

papers 243

paper's 423

parachutes 584, 585, 587, 590, 591, 592, 595, 601

parades 39

paralyzed 243, 394

parboils 581

Parcel Day 211, 241, 267

parched 290, 350

pardoned 423

parents 5, 17, 138, 161, 198, 229, 240, 244, 257, 287, 405, 407, 478, 500, 511, 569, 576, 603

pariahs 130

Parisi 608

parked 605

participating 424

parties 234, 243, 286, 326

partnering 7, 50

partners 6, 371, 521

partway 145

passages 186, 246, 558, 559, 599

passerby 568

passes   56, 121, 157, 186, 200, 241, 255, 265, 284, 376, 377, 451, 493, 518, 558, 598

past   list of   11

patched   434, 455

patches   100, 114, 143, 156, 300, 329, 344, 466, 470, 587

pÃ¢tÃ©   575

pathetically   420

paths   3, 156, 372, 444, 507, 508, 576

patiently   167, 278, 439, 589

patients   146, 267, 271, 342, 431, 447, 454, 456, 459, 474, 476, 477, 527

patient's   516

patrons   491

pats   209, 216, 327, 338, 414, 434, 441

patted   116

pattering   350

patterned   228, 336

patterns   64, 91, 223

patting   186, 416, 487, 529

pauses   130, 241, 330, 333, 427, 463, 480, 522

pausing   27, 55, 80, 114, 385, 605

paved   32

pawing   17, 121

pawns   412, 591

paws   175, 176, 292, 482

paying   155, 160, 454, 459, 483, 525

Paylor   448, 449, 452, 453, 589, 591, 601

pays   58, 256

peacefully   292

peacefulness   365

Peacekeeper   20, 203, 231, 253, 254, 256, 268, 269, 271, 273, 332, 536, 545, 568, 581

Peacekeepers   3, 5, 7, 16, 17, 19, 22, 109, 112, 142, 148, 228, 231, 232, 234, 236, 245, 250, 251, 255, 258, 261, 262, 265, 266, 267, 272, 276, 277, 278, 279, 280, 281, 288, 292, 294, 334, 402, 445, 446, 470, 490, 502, 504, 512, 531, 532, 533, 538, 550, 553, 555, 564, 567, 568, 571, 574, 577, 579, 580, 581, 583, 584, 585, 587, 588

Peacekeeper's   269, 270

Peacekeepers   idea of   578

Peacekeepers   ranks of   503

Peacekeepers   squad of   564

Peacekeeping   316

Peacemakers   235

peaches   579

pearls   40, 186, 283, 326, 328, 387

pears   136

peas   35, 187, 311

peas   size of   42

pebbles   167

pecking 34

peeking 106, 193, 266, 551, 580

peeks 408

peeled 132

peels 346

peering 17, 418, 438, 508, 566, 569

peers 160

Peeta 19, 24, 26, 27, 30, 31, 32, 33, 36, 37, 38, 39, 41, 42, 43, 44, 45, 46, 47, 48, 49, 50, 51, 52, 53, 54, 57, 58, 59, 61, 62, 66, 70, 71, 72, 73, 74, 75, 76, 79, 80, 81, 84, 85, 86, 87, 88, 89, 90, 96, 97, 98, 100, 101, 103, 104, 105, 109, 110, 111, 113, 115, 128, 130, 131, 132, 133, 134, 135, 136, 137, 138, 139, 140, 141, 142, 143, 144, 145, 146, 147, 148, 149, 151, 152, 154, 155, 156, 157, 158, 159, 160, 161, 162, 163, 164, 165, 166, 167, 168, 169, 170, 171, 172, 173, 174, 175, 176, 177, 178, 179, 180, 181, 182, 183, 184, 185, 186, 188, 189, 190, 191, 192, 193, 194, 195, 196, 197, 202, 203, 204, 205, 206, 207, 208, 210, 211, 212, 213, 214, 215, 217, 218, 220, 221, 223, 224, 225, 226, 227, 228, 229, 230, 231, 232, 233, 234, 235, 236, 237, 238, 239, 240, 241, 242, 243, 244, 245, 247, 248, 250, 251, 252, 253, 255, 256, 257, 258, 259, 260, 261, 263, 264, 265, 266, 267, 271, 272, 275, 278, 279, 280, 281, 282, 284, 288, 289, 290, 292, 293, 294, 295, 296, 297, 298, 299, 301, 302, 303, 304, 305, 306, 307, 308, 309, 310, 311, 312, 313, 314, 315, 316, 317, 318, 319, 320, 321, 322, 323, 324, 325, 327, 329, 330, 331, 332, 333, 335, 336, 337, 338, 339, 340, 341, 342, 343, 344, 345, 346, 347, 348, 349, 350, 351, 352, 353, 354, 355, 356, 357, 358, 359, 360, 361, 362, 363, 364, 365, 366, 367, 368, 370, 371, 372, 373, 375, 376, 377, 378, 379, 380, 381, 382, 383, 384, 385, 386, 387, 388, 389, 390, 391, 392, 393, 394, 395, 396, 397, 398, 399, 400, 402, 405, 406, 407, 412, 413, 414, 415, 416, 417, 418, 419, 421, 422, 423, 432, 435, 440, 441, 442, 445, 450, 456, 462, 463, 465, 469, 470, 472, 473, 474, 475, 478, 479, 481, 482, 483, 485, 486, 487, 488, 489, 490, 492, 493, 494, 495, 496, 497, 498, 499, 500, 501, 502, 503, 504, 505, 506, 507, 510, 512, 513, 515, 516, 519, 522, 524, 525, 527, 528, 529, 530, 531, 532, 538, 540, 541, 542, 543, 544, 545, 547, 548, 550, 552, 553, 554, 555, 557, 558, 559, 560, 561, 562, 563, 565, 566, 567, 568, 570, 572, 573, 574, 575, 576, 577, 578, 579, 580, 583, 590, 591, 596, 597, 601, 603, 604, 606, 607, 608

Peeta I'm 337

Peeta Mellark 14, 15, 16, 18, 22, 23, 24, 27, 32, 33, 71, 76, 104, 182, 202, 213, 478

Peeta Mellark's 20, 27

Peeta sight of 266, 325

Peeta sound of 86

Peeta| 396, 462

Peeta|in 324

Peeta|Peeta 189

Peeta's 25, 26, 27, 37, 39, 43, 46, 49, 50, 52, 57, 61, 70, 73, 84, 88, 89, 103, 120, 125, 127, 130, 131, 132, 134, 135, 137, 138, 139, 140, 141, 145, 149, 153, 156, 157, 158, 159, 160, 162, 165, 166, 168, 170, 171, 172, 173, 175, 176, 177, 178, 179, 180, 182, 183, 186, 188, 191, 192, 193, 194, 195, 197, 209, 213, 214, 220, 223, 233, 237, 241, 243, 250, 254, 264, 267, 284, 285, 289, 307, 309, 316, 319, 321, 323, 325, 327, 329, 341, 342, 343, 350, 351, 352, 353, 355, 358, 359, 360, 361, 369, 372, 373, 376, 377, 379, 380, 381, 382, 383, 387, 389, 393, 399, 405, 407, 412, 414, 415, 417, 418, 419, 421, 462, 463, 464, 468, 472, 473, 475, 478, 481, 483, 489, 490, 494, 495, 496, 497, 498, 500, 501, 504, 513, 519, 520, 521, 523, 530, 540, 543, 544, 545,

548, 549, 550, 553, 554, 561, 562, 566, 567, 568, 570, 571, 575, 578, 579, 587, 596, 599, 603, 606

Peeta's Games	544	
Peeta's bottom of	195	
Peeta's pressure of	196	
Peeta's sight of	568	
Peeta's top of	342	
peevishly	164, 441	
pelts	570, 571	
pelts smell of	569	
penalties severest of	3	
penciling	432	
pencils	417	
penetrated	451	
penned	584	
pens	405, 501, 522	
people crush of	599	
people list of	603	
people moaning of	448	
people niceness of	586	
people semicircle of	487	
people throngs of	243	
people's	222, 294, 298, 430, 431, 509, 605, 608	
peppered	473	
peppering	353	
peppermints	278, 279	
perceived	72	
perceptions	528	
perched	9, 27, 100, 127, 128, 174, 374, 395, 441, 467	
perches	111	
Perching	376	
perfected	206	
performed	486, 540	
performers	239	
performs	595	
perfumes	214	
perils	70	
periodically	121, 191, 498, 559, 587	
periods	295, 482, 585	
perks	606	
permeates	548	
perplexing	115, 165	
persists	199, 300, 497	
person sort of	305	
personalities	293	

person's		84, 606
persuaded		146, 417
pervades		104
petals	28, 594	
Peter Bakalian		609
petrified		37, 183
pets	187, 326, 433	
petting		201
photocopying		609
photographs		83
photos	380, 418, 548, 568, 581	
phrases		62
physically		148, 475
picking		31, 49, 205, 224, 286, 318, 320, 338, 513, 533, 561, 580
picks	44, 58, 123, 210, 240, 314, 367, 368, 374, 377, 471, 553	
Picnics		161
pictured		48
pictures		28, 239, 281, 285, 323, 568
picturing		334
pieces	33, 71, 142, 154, 156, 253, 378, 400, 413, 457, 481, 544, 583, 593	
pierced		447
pigs	239	
pig's	55, 57, 172, 241	
Pigs	501	
pillars	207, 503, 512	
pillows		20, 184
pills	135, 136, 137, 140, 223, 236, 237, 446, 554, 594, 600	
pinches		341, 521
pinching		395, 589
pine bundle of		536
pine layer of		82
pines	27, 80	
piney	79	
pinkness		587
pinks	32	
pinned	51, 234, 451, 461	
pinning		77, 113, 150, 390
pinpoints		567
pins	9, 51, 55, 72, 216, 261, 547, 579	
pipes	33, 410, 559	
pitched		24, 87, 103, 123, 176, 358, 538, 552, 568
pitied	49	
pits	115	
pitting	11	
placed	15, 99, 106, 117, 156, 199, 227, 237, 257, 311, 379, 388, 475, 562, 596, 599	

placing		5, 137, 139, 248, 354, 471, 498, 596
plagued		503
plainly	426	
plaintively		155
plaited	16, 347	
planes	400, 451, 453, 455, 458, 471, 510	
planned		86, 212, 234, 262, 279, 302, 322, 421, 459, 519, 521, 563, 572
planning		39, 41, 76, 109, 208, 242, 251, 268, 291, 362, 399, 455, 541
plans		36, 61, 134, 207, 222, 225, 252, 292, 326, 397, 398, 400, 402, 412, 472, 511, 528, 579, 601
plan's	50	
planted		16, 191, 340
plants		14, 27, 28, 51, 52, 54, 60, 91, 96, 100, 132, 133, 134, 167, 238, 278, 281, 347, 353, 357, 364, 369, 384, 407, 430, 436, 498, 557, 576, 589
plants book of		411
plaques		196
plastering		182
plastic sheet of		80, 168
plastic square of		154
plates		29, 47, 116, 161, 165, 227, 300, 334, 335, 338, 578, 593
platform's		197
platters		42, 48, 239
playact		544
played		23, 189, 225, 247, 268, 395, 397, 438, 473, 500, 547, 590, 591, 599, 607
players		22, 58, 59, 76, 81, 94, 129, 299, 300, 301
playing		64, 68, 86, 130, 160, 183, 191, 192, 204, 218, 245, 275, 278, 309, 343, 346, 354, 375, 413, 437, 509, 510, 553, 579
playing size of		604
plays		39, 70, 89, 91, 127, 179, 230, 286, 308, 331, 382, 415, 417, 431, 491, 555
pleadingly		374
pleads	477	
pleasantly		53
pleased		13, 52, 147, 171, 182, 196, 214, 242, 308, 310, 314, 320, 339, 379, 439, 465, 522, 528
pleasures		410
pledged		230
plodding		580
plotted		88
plotting		504
plows	473	
plucked		27, 33, 106, 152, 223, 555
plucking		505
plucks	5	
plugged		185
plugging		41

plugs   517
plummeting   141
plummets   14, 178
plums   60, 61, 68, 223, 555
plunged   196
plunges   337, 598
plunking   485
plunks   517
Plus I've   108
Plutarch   241, 242, 367, 396, 397, 398, 409, 412, 421, 422, 423, 424, 425, 426, 427, 428, 429, 434, 436, 437, 439, 440, 441, 442, 443, 445, 446, 450, 451, 452, 454, 456, 458, 459, 460, 462, 463, 465, 469, 471, 472, 475, 476, 484, 487, 489, 491, 492, 493, 495, 496, 497, 500, 501, 502, 504, 519, 520, 521, 522, 524, 532, 533, 534, 535, 537, 539, 544, 549, 550, 569, 572, 573, 576, 592, 594, 596, 598, 601, 602
Plutarch Heavensbee   241, 316, 345, 395, 396, 397, 402, 406
Plutarch Heavensbee's   320, 321, 367
Plutarch's   407, 424, 451, 465, 473, 475, 488, 490, 497, 503, 520, 521, 538, 539, 569, 572, 590, 593, 597, 602
poaches   255
poaching   3, 108, 254, 266
pockets   568, 587
pockmarked   268
pods   534, 538, 539, 544, 548, 550, 551, 554, 556, 557, 558, 559, 560, 573, 576, 584
pod's   581
pointy   26
poisoned   77, 291, 492
poisons   94, 301
poked   235
pokes   369, 399, 478
poking   119, 146
poles   6
polishes   97
politically   293
Pollux   456, 457, 466, 467, 469, 486, 545, 546, 548, 550, 558, 559, 560, 561, 562, 563, 564, 565, 566, 567, 568, 570, 571, 572, 578, 579, 580, 583, 587
Pollux's   467, 559, 564
pondering   27, 280
ponds   59, 173, 239, 345
pooled   140
pools   132, 566
Poor Effie   312
Poor Finnick   361
Poor Peeta   500
poorest   108, 521
popped   77

popping		108, 278, 344, 360
pores	604	
poring	27, 465	
Portia		36, 37, 39, 41, 43, 54, 57, 58, 66, 71, 72, 73, 74, 185, 186, 190, 193, 196, 220, 224, 232, 235, 241, 243, 304, 307, 308, 311, 312, 321, 322, 327, 333, 497
Portia's		191, 308
portions		187, 349, 420
portrayed		422
portraying		309
poses	62	
positioned		149, 272, 338, 369, 392, 409, 438, 514, 545, 589
positioning		79, 150, 546
positions		37, 188, 225, 259, 352, 357, 428, 442, 453, 546, 576
possessions		362, 366, 527
possessively		361
possibilities		115, 556, 577, 591
Possibly Peeta		26
possum's		98
posted	476	
posts	405	
Posy|	376	
potatoes		25, 30, 58, 304, 312, 528, 577
potentially		293
pounces		318
pounding		38, 67, 96, 178, 191, 192, 200, 290, 312, 581
pounds		25, 51, 54, 65, 97, 105, 352, 395, 462, 500
poured		18, 189, 215, 292
pouring		153, 163, 175, 298, 302, 450, 511, 526, 565, 581, 584
pours		202, 209, 237, 256, 355, 373
poverty	noose of	288
power centers of	272	
power's		482
practicing		60, 159, 325
Praised Fulvia		460
prattling		586
pre	191	
prearranged		149
precariously		99, 233, 276
precautions		110, 437
precedes		66, 126, 395
predators		3, 6, 82, 120, 123, 200, 605
predawn		575
Predictably		323
predicted		514
predicting		532

Predictions   293
predicts   555, 575
prefers   344
prep   33, 34, 39, 64, 65, 105, 187, 188, 190, 193, 199, 214, 216, 217, 222, 223, 228, 234, 235, 236, 240, 243, 303, 304, 315, 325, 326, 426, 428, 429, 430, 431, 433, 434, 435, 436, 439, 440, 465, 485, 491, 497, 520, 555, 594, 595, 596
preparations   76, 148, 350, 532, 541
prepares   135
preparing   169, 198, 217, 248, 275, 284, 337, 412, 477, 531, 588, 602
prepped   183, 245, 490
prepping   223, 244
preps   218, 428, 434, 435
prescribes   240
preserved   77, 408, 607
preserves   47
preserving   83, 509
presided   41, 211
President Coin   510, 540, 549, 556, 586, 587, 598
President Coin's   428, 549
President Coriolanus Snow   492
President Snow   192, 193, 194, 207, 208, 209, 210, 213, 218, 219, 220, 221, 222, 225, 231, 233, 234, 237, 238, 239, 243, 245, 247, 251, 252, 258, 260, 264, 268, 275, 276, 286, 288, 293, 299, 308, 310, 312, 322, 323, 326, 327, 328, 329, 335, 343, 368, 394, 408, 412, 433, 454, 455, 458, 481, 490, 491, 499, 509, 544, 549, 556, 561, 587, 588, 590, 603
President Snow's   39, 208, 210, 212, 220, 223, 224, 238, 248, 280, 288, 324, 326, 399, 403, 409, 417, 472, 550
presidential   538
presidents   209, 590
president's   193, 212, 213, 221, 248, 250, 424, 567, 574, 580, 584, 587, 588, 598
pressed   2, 182, 212, 301, 305, 322, 354, 379, 429, 511, 514, 548, 566
presses   7, 35, 107, 139, 162, 184, 221, 231, 236, 304, 376, 414, 425, 437, 438, 462, 506, 511, 520, 536, 581
pressingly   37
pressured   387
pretending   50, 61, 87, 207, 296, 379, 465, 483, 604
pretends   314, 602
prettying   430
prevented   518
preventing   183
prevents   74
previously   281, 606
prey|that's   437
preying   236
prices   568
pricey   89

pried 205, 387
pries 558
Prim opposite of 111
Prim|did Peeta 33
Prim|Rue|aren't 262
primroses 605
Prim's 2, 9, 14, 16, 18, 19, 27, 28, 124, 127, 142, 143, 144, 150, 185, 201, 222, 249, 278, 279, 291, 295, 374, 376, 377, 421, 441, 477, 478, 480, 498, 511, 565, 606
Prim's crook of 418
printed 437
prints 121, 268
priorities 271
prisoners 583
privately 193, 395, 442, 463, 522
privileges 245, 429
prizes 11
probes 47
proceedings 421
proclaimed 272
prodding 31, 103
prods 581
produces 539
producing 460
products 279, 283, 434, 599
professing 84
professionals 497
programmed 177, 416, 504, 549, 561
programming 285, 415, 425, 472, 601
progressively 141
projected 331, 348, 472
projects 236, 533, 556
prominently 312
promised 27, 37, 57, 58, 113, 151, 218, 267, 268, 295, 326, 433, 511
promises 234, 379, 518, 539, 545, 607
promoted 73, 316
prompts 70
pronged 359
propaganda mixture of 282
Propelled 447
propels 338
properties 439
propo 439, 457, 459, 461, 462, 463, 464, 510, 519, 520, 521, 544, 548
propos 425, 438, 460, 462, 465, 472, 473, 485, 504, 510, 513, 531, 540, 541, 568
proposed 587, 597
proposing 249, 252

propped   15, 137, 139, 243, 431, 448, 581, 605
propping   95, 466
props   279, 341, 550
prospects   122
prosthetic   472
protected   110, 407, 575, 596
protective   layers of   517
protectively   158, 461, 513, 522
protects   4, 116
protestations   344
protesting   232
protruding   346, 531
proved   157, 301
proves   143, 554
provides   132, 171, 368, 499, 583
proving   213
provisions   82, 273, 420, 532, 592
provoked   57, 316
provokes   186
pruned   589
pruning   589
Publication Data   609
Publishers   609
puckered   184
puffier   555
puffs   329, 580
puked   540
pulled   9, 13, 28, 37, 60, 63, 102, 124, 129, 176, 188, 195, 208, 219, 275, 322, 404, 406, 492, 542, 569
pulling   13, 25, 32, 35, 38, 95, 102, 111, 124, 126, 127, 164, 166, 177, 179, 181, 182, 194, 195, 197, 213, 220, 228, 243, 324, 351, 370, 375, 394, 414, 481, 499, 515, 518, 565, 566
pulls   5, 12, 20, 21, 27, 33, 49, 58, 72, 77, 107, 113, 153, 158, 163, 165, 179, 180, 183, 189, 194, 195, 205, 224, 238, 240, 242, 248, 249, 254, 261, 287, 290, 297, 298, 301, 309, 312, 327, 380, 391, 398, 412, 418, 425, 429, 466, 470, 471, 472, 476, 484, 487, 502, 505, 506, 521, 527, 585, 602
pulsating   474
punches   31
punctured   514
punctures   150, 337
punished   18, 189, 193, 233, 267, 282, 349, 395, 412, 427, 463
punishing   214, 428, 431, 432, 542
pupils   254, 271, 358, 374, 566, 567
puppetlike   352
puppets   538
purchases   203

pureed 295
purer 588
purges 355
purification 472
purified 444
purifying 91, 141
Purnia 255, 256
Purnia's 255
purposefully 150
purposes 382
purring 411, 598
purrs 151
purses 526
pursued 288, 374
pursuers 80, 96
pursues 409
pursuing 94, 262, 338
pushes 48, 190, 220, 232, 251, 254, 341, 400, 416, 451, 493, 494, 546, 553, 569, 572, 599
putrefying 448
putting 48, 80, 101, 108, 117, 231, 242, 367, 490, 497, 499, 508, 542, 570, 592
puzzled 146, 302, 344, 363, 427
puzzles 119, 545
puzzling 79, 594
qualities 498
quarries 445, 446
Quarter Quell 217, 286, 287, 288, 291, 294, 297, 298, 299, 326, 328, 381, 394, 404, 417, 425, 431, 444, 483, 489, 507, 517, 535, 555, 562, 579, 594, 599
Quarter Quell Games 242
Quarter Quell|well 412, 575
Quarter Quells 286
quarts 143
questioned 454
questioningly 205, 467
questions 53, 63, 64, 66, 113, 157, 184, 185, 190, 194, 214, 237, 238, 243, 328, 347, 397, 411, 484, 494, 508, 545, 551, 601, 607, 609
question's 162
Questions 473
quickening 4
quickens 364
quicker 10, 357
quickest 433, 564
quieter 69, 167, 171, 233, 319, 343
quiets 585
quitting 112, 174

quivering 283
quizzically 452
quizzing 531
quotas 108
rabbits 28, 48, 59, 60, 82, 91, 168, 170, 172, 200, 430
rabbit's 170
races 79
Rachel Coun 608
racketeers 10
racking 15
racks 232, 569, 606
radiates 249, 298, 528, 563
radiating 83, 263, 335
rages 8
raging 76, 566
rain   lack of 430
rain   memories of 555
rain   sound of 153
rainbow   piles of 539
rainbows 112
raindrops 478
raining 404, 478
rain's 366
raises 46, 57, 69, 99, 169, 178, 181, 184, 230, 247, 252, 385, 392, 432, 466, 474, 477,
606, 607
raisins 18, 154
raking 600
rallied 465
rallying 406, 540
rambles 146
ramblings 411
rammed 546
ranches 405
randomly 372
ranges 436
ranks 405, 424
rapidly 139, 339, 432, 462, 474, 476, 534, 543, 547, 567
raspberries 239
ratcheting 141
rats 2, 376, 384, 386, 559, 571
rat's 349
ratted 459
rattled 423
rattles 190, 243, 541
ravaged 594

ravings 125

rawness 586

rays 98, 127, 174, 274

razzle 522

reached 18, 79, 80, 96, 116, 175, 178, 302, 338, 351, 354, 441, 452, 459, 523, 547, 551

reaches 12, 80, 116, 124, 152, 176, 319, 329, 338, 339, 348, 391, 395, 400, 403, 424, 441, 449, 451, 484, 488, 502, 534, 549, 558, 573, 578

reaching 162, 195, 331, 337, 341, 373, 374, 375, 419, 495, 514

reacted 250

reacting 67, 493, 563

reactivating 453

reacts 67, 287, 307, 330, 492

readied 150, 234, 532, 577

reads 11, 12, 177, 287, 299, 476, 555, 587

readying 61, 131, 362

realization 17, 331, 383, 428, 452, 482

realize|he 129

realized 42, 49, 154, 157, 244, 299, 330, 361, 414, 561, 583

realized|I 507

realizes 52, 147, 178, 352

realizing 144, 514, 542

really|I'm 415

reaped 287, 288, 595

reaping 2, 3, 4, 6, 7, 8, 9, 11, 13, 15, 30, 33, 46, 47, 69, 70, 144, 160, 162, 165, 191, 196, 211, 218, 221, 222, 227, 237, 244, 246, 248, 249, 250, 259, 286, 288, 290, 291, 294, 296, 378, 418, 441, 585, 605

reapings 11, 13, 25, 296, 299

reaping's 294

reappearance 136, 290, 594

reappears 119, 571

rearranged 571

reasons 63, 285, 373, 443, 522, 525, 539, 590

reassurance 70

reassurances 69

reassured 168, 281, 561, 570

reassures 69, 381

reassuring 19, 193, 194, 206, 235, 291, 293, 537

reattaches 518

rebel   help of 493

rebelled 597

rebelling 283, 285, 286

rebellion   fire of 425

rebellion   flames of 433

rebellions 251

rebellion's 251

rebels 24, 32, 99, 246, 272, 285, 286, 287, 288, 295, 324, 335, 343, 394, 402, 403, 407, 408, 410, 412, 413, 414, 415, 416, 417, 419, 422, 432, 433, 442, 446, 450, 452, 454, 457, 458, 461, 462, 463, 465, 473, 474, 492, 503, 512, 513, 514, 515, 516, 518, 519, 531, 532, 538, 539, 544, 549, 551, 553, 555, 556, 568, 573, 574, 575, 576, 579, 581, 584, 588, 591, 592, 595, 596

rebounded 285, 563

rebounds 96

recalling 418

recalls 328

recaps 293

recedes 312, 452, 515

receding 546

received 56, 59, 233, 302, 304, 305, 381, 397, 407, 532, 609

receives 11, 168, 411

Receiving 528

recent indentations of 268

recesses 478

recites 328

recognizable 38, 426, 439

recognized 59, 127, 169, 347, 512, 568, 583

recognizes 107, 438, 537, 567

recognizing 343, 501

recommended 532

recommending 541

reconciliation 516

reconstructed 344, 356, 385

Reconstructing 544

recorded 24, 220, 376, 423, 454, 606

recordings 292

records 219, 497

recounts 507

recovered 111, 170, 177, 241, 242, 429

recovering 111, 114

recovers 355, 460, 482

recreational 268

recruiting 446

recuperating 418, 525

reddened 254

redder 590

redesign 372

redesigned 425

redheaded 46, 47, 61, 64, 74, 76, 87, 184, 185, 270, 310, 311, 324, 507

redheads 545

redirect 194

redone 574

redressed 81
redresses 579
reduces 521
reeking 403
reeks 14, 208
reeling 358, 549
reels 462
reenact 466
reenacting 546
reenactments 77
refasten 83
referencing 282
referred 77, 576
referring 86, 144
refers 228
refills 89, 418
refineries 236
reflected 300, 409
reflecting 139, 184
reflects 82, 309, 449, 560, 587
reflexively 80, 178, 425, 581
refreshed 106, 496
refugees 402, 403, 409, 420, 520, 576, 577, 578, 579, 580, 581, 582, 584
refugees wave of 577
refused 12, 187, 403, 440
refuses 88, 137, 139, 204, 301, 365
refusing 49, 89, 145, 225, 557
regained 116, 177, 363, 395, 553
regaining 120, 257
regains 39
regions 24
registering 15, 560
registers 94, 97, 207, 394, 464, 604
regretfully 160
regretted 4
regretting 224, 413
regroup 97, 519, 552
regrouped 538
regulating 41
rehydrate 96, 601
reinforced 426, 463, 503
reinforcements 424
reinforces 157, 570
reinsert 399
reinstated 473

reinvent 519
reinvents 217
rejected 68
rejecting 9, 579
rejoins 323, 359
rejuvenating 81, 528
relapses 461
relates 232
relatively 37, 83, 96, 140, 404
relatives 455, 511
relaxed 122, 325
relaxes 43, 120
relaxing 4
relayed 503
released 24, 178, 209, 287, 463, 479, 481, 499, 510, 547, 562, 587, 590
releases 14, 51, 76, 78, 125, 178, 314, 358, 359, 429, 453
releasing 295, 544, 581
relents 313
reliability 554
reliably 233
relieved 24, 37, 59, 61, 84, 171, 295, 314, 432, 463, 520, 573, 579
relieves 540
relinquishing 493
reliving 559
reload 337, 370
reloaded 124
relocate 476
relocated 504
reluctantly 145, 412
relying 141
remade 499
remained 10, 92, 223, 609
remaining 85, 94, 122, 147, 179, 180, 257, 271, 293, 296, 301, 382, 387, 388, 394, 403, 430, 536, 574, 579, 581, 585, 587, 596
remaining idea of 525
Remake Center 33, 37, 43, 305
remaking 579
remarkably 91, 216, 261, 293, 338, 594
remarks 76
remedies 5, 29, 135, 256, 267, 587
remembered 59, 212, 512
remembering 21, 242, 279, 286, 323, 347, 361, 387, 400, 590
remembers 2, 49, 314, 385, 515
remembrances 407
reminded 18, 43, 53, 118, 246, 392, 408, 481

reminder		10, 74, 88, 99, 188, 235, 286, 287, 288, 295, 312, 381, 386, 394, 429
reminding		11, 25, 61, 193, 196, 303, 394, 590
reminds		32, 57, 91, 107, 159, 179, 243, 258, 347, 363, 383, 386, 389, 411, 430, 446, 517, 525, 541, 574, 576, 577, 586, 597
remnants		566
remotely		523
removes		206, 287, 494, 529, 551, 590
removing		34, 39, 277, 337
removing	complications of	474
rendered		310, 383
renderings		269
reneging		419
renewed		93
renovations		405
rents	327	
rent's	558	
reoccurring		383
reorganizing		519
repaid	573	
repaired		219
repeatedly		19, 90, 104, 122, 153, 323, 355, 363, 457, 508, 530
repeating		464
repeats		13, 123, 130, 163, 340, 374, 413, 422, 467, 539
repelled		252
repellence		569
repercussions		254, 456
replaced		7, 17, 60, 195, 224, 239, 281, 296, 405, 449, 473, 493, 515, 528, 530
replaces		464, 472, 479
replacing		457
replaying		412, 457, 463
replicated		239
replicating		565
replied	214	
replies	112, 223, 270, 324, 384, 442, 476, 486, 509, 529, 574	
reported		276, 578
reporters		22, 199, 204, 211, 214, 553
reporting		461
reports		224, 282, 429
repositioned		156
representatives		446
representing		346, 369
represents		81, 533
reprieved		59
reproduced		609
reprogramming		606

reptiles	110
repulsed	80, 433
requested	427, 577
requests	339, 553
required	15, 71, 73, 78, 191, 218, 255, 287, 410, 420, 431, 587, 609
requires	.11, 89, 96, 99, 104, 116, 248, 266, 269, 283
reruns	217, 457, 488
rescheduled	265
rescued	399, 406, 450, 523, 540, 603
rescuers	454, 590
resembled	578
resembling	567
resented	212
resentfully	478
reservations	40, 407, 490, 520
resetting	200
reshaped	284
rcsidents	73, 77, 228, 573
resigns	217
resisting	338
resists	170, 293
resolve's	600
resolving	111, 592
resonates	478
resonating	329
resounding	238
resourcefulness	51
resources	157, 292, 410, 471, 503
respected	28, 230
respcctfully	405
responded	45, 72
responding	399, 442, 586
responds	11, 522, 539
response lack of	545
responses	229, 546
responsibilities	519
ress	609
restarted	529
rested	140, 156, 350, 365, 379
restlessly	365
restlessness	122
restoring	356
restraining	184, 548
restraints	396, 501, 502, 521, 522, 571
rests	158, 243, 254, 381, 560, 586

resulted	18, 525
resulting	205, 267
results	22, 122, 407, 474, 496, 562
resumed	211
resumes	205
resuming	212
retained	371
retains	306
retches	548
retching	94
retelling	161
rethinking	310
rethought	188
retinal	437
retorts	509, 597
retracing	571
retracts	447
retreated	583
retreating	236, 334
retrieved	27, 76, 105
retrieves	213
retrieving	34, 97
return|	366
returned	29, 60, 120, 121, 130, 185, 196, 206, 212, 239, 355
returning	75, 93, 214, 223, 274, 303, 326, 341, 402, 452, 465, 504, 506, 508, 524, 558, 569
returns	71, 102, 106, 155, 359, 386, 428, 483, 527, 540, 560, 568
reusing	273
revealed	83, 88, 175
revealing	37, 111, 205, 258, 277, 326, 349, 358, 382, 394, 427, 429, 443, 546, 569, 594
reveals	388
reversed	170, 307, 509
reverting	114
reviewed	525
reviewing	185
reviews	609
revised	496
revisit	221, 543
revived	483
reviving	117, 372
revoked	181, 429
revolted	283
rewarded	87, 133, 321, 537
rewards	308

rewatch 77

rhythmic 158, 356

rhythmic cessation of 543

ribbons 112, 283, 305, 504

ribs 96, 105, 187, 188, 341, 358, 364, 516, 517, 518, 521, 522, 523, 525, 526, 528

Richard Register 609

richest 19, 30

ridding 33, 555

riddled 142, 355, 362, 516

rides 236, 299, 338, 352

ridges 175

ridiculed 108

ridiculously 444

rigged 93, 531

rigidity 70

rigs 222

ringing 119, 120, 121, 310, 391, 393, 546

ringlets 234, 283, 434

rings 79, 131, 258, 264, 374, 534, 569, 603

rinsed 365

rinses 387, 410

rinsing 106, 570

ripening 448

ripped 104, 223, 459, 599

Ripper 203, 265, 267, 284, 292

rippled 386

ripples 434, 451

rippling 316, 341, 449

rips 58, 182, 343, 509, 565, 580

risen 20

rises 21, 31, 35, 54, 88, 99, 150, 165, 213, 225, 227, 292, 297, 300, 307, 348, 365, 415, 431, 461, 508, 543, 558, 585, 586

risked 61, 335, 483, 571

risking 116, 145, 222, 276, 373

risks 474, 538

riveted 530

riveting 159, 308, 490

roads 503

roaming 5, 236, 316, 469

roars 548

roasted 107, 141, 215, 239, 240, 347, 600

robbed 144

robed 375

robes 52, 431

robotic 127

robustness 412
rock tons of 32
rockers 278, 279
rockets 175
Rockies 23
rocking 24, 376, 411, 584, 606
rocks 5, 93, 95, 102, 117, 128, 132, 133, 134, 136, 137, 141, 147, 148, 149, 153, 154, 160, 163, 166, 167, 172, 173, 274, 301, 365, 470, 566
rodents 173, 267
rodent's 347
roles 608
rolled 86, 124, 127, 403
rolls 35, 36, 47, 49, 79, 160, 168, 169, 172, 187, 309, 337, 350, 353, 354, 356, 378, 381, 382, 387, 397, 579
rolls basket of 30
Rome 519
Romulus Thread 256, 404
Rooba 142, 143, 144, 268
rooftops 9, 245, 265, 514, 515, 551, 556
room's 312, 472, 473
roosting 120
rooting 27
roots 5, 17, 28, 29, 91, 92, 96, 108, 112, 120, 128, 138, 141, 156, 168, 170, 172, 215, 226, 434, 478, 604
roped 10, 294
ropes 253, 255, 314, 326, 335
Rory 202, 259, 262, 266, 267, 376
rosebushes 576
Rosemary Stimola 608
roses 70, 194, 207, 283, 421, 486, 487, 490, 492, 531, 563, 588, 589, 604
roses reek of 564
roses smell of 208
rotating 477
rotted 17, 582
rotting 2, 400
rougher 185
roughly 113, 251, 254, 300
rounds 188, 271, 510, 581
roused 28, 73, 236, 325
rouses 30, 280, 325, 381
rowdily 53
rows 287, 395, 449
rubbed 485
rubs 49, 154, 205, 209, 333, 349, 478, 520, 523, 531, 579
Rue I'd 129

Rue   warmth of   111

Rue| 177

Rue|so   84

Rue's   101, 106, 107, 108, 113, 117, 118, 123, 124, 125, 126, 127, 128, 129, 134, 136, 139, 141, 148, 149, 153, 155, 164, 168, 169, 174, 222, 229, 230, 232, 233, 262, 331, 369, 417, 467

Rue's| 229

ruffles   309

ruined   56, 356, 593

ruins   119, 235, 282, 402, 486, 605

ruled   336, 522

rules   8, 11, 31, 51, 71, 76, 130, 153, 227, 234, 315, 324, 395, 420, 430, 431, 577

rumbled   142

rumbling   188, 432

rumblings   285

ruminates   328

ruminating   75

rumored   324

rumors   284, 462, 518

rungs   76, 565

runs   19, 30, 32, 46, 49, 52, 62, 88, 105, 116, 146, 174, 179, 229, 235, 259, 266, 287, 302, 306, 310, 314, 321, 362, 371, 390, 394, 398, 412, 447, 494, 498, 557, 570, 575, 584, 598, 599, 607

ruptured   358, 517

rushes   39, 207, 221, 230, 485, 519

rustily   517

rustles   309

rustling   86, 98, 101, 122

S.S.C   531

s|no   33

sacks   59, 114, 455

sacrificed   40, 166, 543, 591

sacrifices   601

sacrificing   373, 572

sadder   127

sadistic   152, 207, 374

sadly   71, 375

Sae   271

safe| 320

safely   76, 100, 232, 268, 271, 295, 504, 573, 576

safer   94, 96, 411, 480

safest   175, 383

safety   illusion of   293

safety's   504

sagged   352

sagging		308, 358
sags	545	
said|about		501
sailboats		521
Saliva's		487
salivating		306
saltiness		57
saltwater's		340
salvageable		587
salvaged		466
sampled		240
samples		281
sanctioned		23
sandals		187, 191
sandwiches		466
saplings		200
saps	571	
sated	100	
satellites		471
satisfying		321, 368, 380, 554
saturates		585
sauces	239	
sauntered		592
saunters		306
sausages		47
savages		25
saved		104, 105, 106, 110, 143, 144, 153, 165, 222, 257, 260, 290, 344, 360, 472, 486, 496, 543, 571, 586
saves	441	
savoring		161
savvy	608	
sawing		80, 99, 101
say|Snow		492
scabbed		359
scabs	361, 362, 382, 383, 494	
scalding		271
scalds	94	
scaled	585	
scales	97, 382	
scaling	175, 458	
scaling odds of		199
scampering		116
scampers		368
scanning		547, 563
scans	253, 437	

scared	4, 5, 45, 95, 128, 137, 154, 203, 255, 266, 391, 518, 580, 584
scares	8, 56, 165
scarier	352
scarred	248, 425, 447, 594
scars	21, 183, 184, 185, 431, 433, 517, 595, 604
scarves	568
scattered	532
scavenged	16
scavengers	403
scenarios	337
scenes	459
scented	572
scents	41, 207
scheduled	285, 319, 415, 421, 436, 451, 463, 521
schedules	437, 504
Scholastic Inc	609
SCHOLASTIC PRESS	1, 198, 401
schoolchildren	385, 429
schools	387
school's	501
sci	609
scooped	507
scooping	53, 420, 555
scoops	31, 280, 338, 419, 455, 506
scoots	435, 518
scopes	438
scorched	17, 92, 96, 405
scorching	403, 430
scored	68, 79
scores	56, 57, 58, 83, 191, 323, 356, 584
scoring	56
scoured	223
scouts	576
scowled	60
scowling	220, 333
scowls	521, 550, 596
scrambled	79
scrambling	152, 433, 510, 565, 582
scraped	18, 201, 273
scrapes	550, 604
scraping	67, 82, 146, 176, 370, 604
scraps	109, 408, 468
scratched	591
scratching	360
screaming	3, 13, 17, 47, 94, 103, 151, 171, 183, 192, 203, 237, 245, 263, 286, 297,

334, 362, 374, 398, 406, 450, 454, 521, 523, 531, 582, 594, 599, 607

screams 65, 71, 103, 328, 363, 375, 529, 531, 533, 546, 562, 563, 565, 569, 580

screeches 152

screens 10, 127, 129, 148, 308, 331, 351, 413, 457, 472, 482, 493, 499, 513, 514, 599

scribbles 526

scribbling 450

scripted 228, 229

scrounged 27

scrubbed 184, 448

scrubbing 33

scrupulously 131

scrutinizing 372

scuffling 84, 576

scurrying 173

seafood's 384

sealing 479

seals 183, 521

seal's 119, 127, 473

seams 175

searches 116, 222, 451

seared 94

searing 90, 92, 263, 351, 353, 451

seas 10

seasons 60

seated 33, 70, 555

seats 67, 243, 435, 455

seawater 339, 355, 356, 362, 364, 370, 385, 585

secretly 41, 162, 174, 187, 199, 468, 501

secrets 211, 216, 233, 306, 307, 400, 416, 419, 491, 494

secret's 242

Secrets 491

sectioned 366

sections 281, 370, 510

secured 99, 272, 371, 388, 538, 576, 589

securely 297, 334, 350

secures 45, 443, 446, 579, 595

securing 131, 170, 228, 281, 576

security sense of 154

sedated 99

see|I 430

Seeder's 348

seeds 53, 127, 239, 607

seeing idea of 196

seeing joy of 415

seeing   shock of   207
seeking   2, 178, 454, 485, 561, 571, 587
seemingly   44
seeped   449
seeping   5, 185
seeps   78, 262, 599
segue   195, 329
seized   153, 353
selected   505, 537
selects   151, 315
selfpity   380
seller's   580
selling   3, 19, 258
sells   6, 21, 31, 48, 255, 568
semiconsciousness   395
sending   31, 90, 93, 117, 138, 141, 156, 171, 206, 246, 261, 292, 385, 391, 417,
431, 454, 455, 458, 488, 489, 505, 517, 518, 554, 565, 572, 575
sending   idea of   442
sends   41, 92, 94, 115, 118, 127, 141, 150, 180, 187, 193, 224, 233, 259, 304, 318, 331,
460, 481, 482, 526, 552, 576, 590, 594
Seneca Crane   208, 242, 321
Seneca Crane's   322
sensations   506
sensation's   361, 381
sensed   172
senses   89, 104, 114, 120, 205, 274, 275, 315, 357, 381, 426, 448, 565
sensibly   37
Sensing   336
Sensors   479
sentenced   256, 469, 588
sentences   33
sentencing   193, 395
separated   71, 108
separately   48, 50, 61, 438
separating   3, 32
September   485
seriously   87, 265, 310, 438
servants   545
served   30, 41, 42, 53, 122, 228, 234, 321, 429, 457, 590
servers   42, 311
serves   58, 203, 239, 255
services   267, 539
servings   162
sets   38, 42, 86, 179, 184, 205, 209, 240, 249, 298, 325, 361, 363, 367, 379, 382, 404,
420, 422, 447, 476, 487, 546, 601

settings 187

settled 16, 211, 478, 483, 485

settles 71, 192, 326, 350, 396, 397, 402, 412, 505, 575

severed 61, 389

severely 14, 463, 539

severing 382, 589

sewers 559

shackled 426, 529, 571

shackles 427, 428, 589

shacks 227

shade bit of 368

shaded 228, 229

shades 126, 225

shadow protection of 514

shadows 122, 123, 261, 304, 362, 492, 512, 543, 582

shafts 287, 448, 510, 559, 605

shaken 342, 377

shakes 42, 64, 71, 107, 118, 142, 145, 172, 177, 183, 204, 251, 252, 298, 302, 310, 348, 427, 446, 465, 486, 489, 506, 522, 533, 541, 548, 554, 559, 566, 573, 574, 591

shakier 417

shakily 52

shallowness 570

shallows 215, 356, 364

shampoos 41

shapes 33, 551

shards 71, 483

shared 211, 249, 299, 402

shares 500

sharing 43, 179, 223, 317, 410, 508

sharpens 114

sharply 119, 278, 339, 473, 478

sharpshooters 533, 535, 537

sharpshooter's 539

shattered 118, 119, 212, 289, 560, 593

shattering 539

shatters 31, 71, 103, 233, 546

shaved 254, 283, 447, 494, 517

sheepishly 137

sheeting's 288

sheets 16, 29, 56, 64, 460, 586, 593, 606

sheets pressure of 586

Sheila Marie Everett 608

shells 346, 355, 360, 377, 388, 447, 456, 466, 511, 553, 558

sheltered 166, 584

sheltering 93

shelters 115
She's Finnick Odair's 432
She's Finnick's 432
shielding 451
shields 360, 452
shifted 11, 359, 372
shifting 124, 147, 341, 522, 534, 571
shifts 166, 270, 336, 447, 559, 586, 598
shimmering 234, 341, 362, 392
shimmers 65, 359
shines 99, 259
shining 10, 62, 294, 335
shipments 528
shipped 81
shirtfront 317
shirts 51
shirtsleeve 205
shirttail 205
shivering 45, 46, 137, 158, 261, 270, 495, 572, 580
shock look of 321
shock waves of 491
shocked 58, 152, 216, 344, 405, 602
shocks 462, 535
shoelaces 6, 544
shoes 9, 26, 34, 46, 47, 62, 65, 187, 193, 201, 206, 217, 224, 234, 266, 283, 284, 326, 333, 354, 402, 416, 430, 451, 472, 567, 568
shoos 193, 383
shooting 39, 55, 56, 57, 91, 150, 241, 318, 319, 337, 357, 367, 393, 394, 417, 422, 451, 492, 517, 524, 527, 536, 541, 552, 581, 596, 600
shootings 234
shoots 7, 49, 60, 80, 98, 101, 209, 259, 296, 302, 351, 352, 444, 472, 529, 539, 581
shopkeepers 164, 577
shops 9, 16, 277, 402, 405, 569, 580
shopwindows 581
shortages 4, 267, 284, 415
shorter 392
shortest 293
shots 81, 83, 111, 192, 232, 237, 245, 286, 346, 451, 453, 458, 473, 496, 532, 533, 538, 546, 577, 581
shouldered 21, 23
shoulders 3, 14, 15, 29, 41, 45, 54, 72, 80, 96, 106, 150, 156, 168, 186, 192, 196, 201, 234, 249, 250, 298, 326, 330, 332, 349, 390, 404, 406, 424, 447, 511, 513, 559
should've 435, 477, 483
shouted 194
shouting 38, 70, 84, 119, 148, 177, 351, 452, 455, 458, 490, 494, 565, 581

shouts		14, 38, 55, 69, 148, 152, 182, 216, 352, 358, 375, 377, 453, 502, 553, 565, 584
shoved		18, 71, 73, 281, 565
shoveled		61
Shoveling		605
shovels		265
shoves		103, 220, 362, 363
shoving		182, 231, 390, 477, 510, 563
shoving	risk of	92
showered		11, 531
showering		38, 480
showers		70, 91, 394, 535
showier		438
showtime		206
shredded		257, 566, 599
shrieking		94, 102, 174, 184, 331, 357, 565
shrieks		216, 240, 321, 374, 475, 478, 510
shrinking		174, 601
shrinks		81, 477
Shriveled		604
shrugged		143
shrugs		21, 33, 49, 61, 73, 300, 488, 507, 545, 573, 602
shuffling		427, 577
shunned		260
shuts		192, 213, 333, 351, 494, 527
shutters		3, 6, 29, 158, 160, 266, 552, 573, 576, 577, 579, 580, 604
shutting		299, 324, 497, 542
Shutting Prim		419
shyly	218	
shyness		39
siblings		112, 229, 511
sick	parade of	291
sickened		33, 334
sickeningly		351, 486
side's	275	
sidestepped		214
sideswiped		494
sidetracked		241
Sifting	605	
sighing		365
sighs		70, 134, 149, 223, 289, 296, 319, 424, 455, 517, 561
sighting		282
sightings		578
sights		137, 254, 453
signaled		230
signaling		20

signals   102, 112, 168, 274, 381, 386, 410, 421, 484, 524, 539
signed   28, 201, 267, 399
significant   destruction of   539
significantly   601
signifies   56, 275
signifying   90
signing   73, 267, 520
signs   85, 86, 89, 122, 141, 166, 167, 195, 268, 276, 409, 455, 475, 550, 557
silences   85, 238
silencing   582
silently   9, 98, 123, 164, 197, 356, 421, 426, 453, 457, 498, 563
silhouettes   55
silk   circle of   348
silliest   240
silly|but   480
simpleminded   86, 87, 109
simpler   207, 285, 327
simplest   127, 402
Simulated Street Combat   531
simultaneously   155, 265, 585
sincerely   34, 460
singed   341, 588
singed   scent of   94
singeing   596
singing   29, 44, 57, 75, 98, 113, 123, 141, 149, 218, 368, 369, 370, 468, 469, 512, 513, 602, 606
singling   320
sings   112, 127, 586
sings|even   159
sinks   51, 70, 130, 181, 271, 336, 347, 352, 357, 358, 389, 424, 565
sinuses   355
siphoning   517
sipped   91
sipping   91, 149, 213, 292, 333
sips   78, 104, 271, 284, 436
sirens   451, 474, 475, 477, 478, 510, 511, 568
sisters   230, 232, 537, 595, 609
sister's   29, 69, 148, 201, 542, 591
sites   77, 267
sits   2, 19, 21, 24, 29, 30, 31, 93, 114, 128, 134, 140, 150, 165, 171, 205, 213, 233, 257, 270, 279, 280, 291, 300, 302, 342, 348, 359, 360, 370, 381, 397, 409, 411, 419, 428, 436, 483, 486, 487, 488, 500, 542, 560, 569, 573, 584, 603, 606
sixteen   age of   8
sixteens   10
sizes   176, 269

skating	206
skeletal	358
sketchbooks	218, 219
sketches	281, 325, 425
skewers	55, 347
skidding	533
skids	94
skies	86
skills	48, 51, 52, 56, 293, 314, 319, 322, 482
skills|was	61
skin layers of	352
skinning	346, 430
skins	88
skin's	185, 589
skipped	222
skipping	298
skips	207, 512
skirts	301
skunks	470
skylights	448
sky's	111, 394, 451
slabs	503
slammed	53, 435, 565
slamming	292, 371, 510, 548
slams	50, 55, 150, 178, 277, 289, 548, 566, 584, 599
slanting	174, 281
slapped	457
slapping	58, 341
slaps	203, 363, 452, 458, 485, 525
slashes	103, 205
slated	54, 464, 538
slaughtered	303
slaves	250, 454, 503, 515, 556
sleep influence of	516
sleep tendrils of	280
sleepily	165
sleepless circles of	443
sleeps	205, 223, 293, 586
Sleep's	526
sleeved	47
sleeveless	188
sleeves	283, 284, 326, 328, 329, 424, 434
slenderest	97, 219
slept	30, 84, 172, 173, 243, 261, 313, 456, 571
sliced	18, 42, 369

slices 5, 18, 47, 150, 164, 205, 581
slid 17, 277, 569
slides 90, 98, 154, 184, 186, 334, 348, 380, 395, 413, 415, 418, 424, 435, 457, 515, 570, 572, 573
slightest 54, 65, 126, 202, 295, 354, 598
sliminess 387, 435
slimmest 227
slings 550
Slinking 268
slinks 347, 569
slipped 142, 149, 279, 283, 288
slippers 220, 221, 309, 443, 576, 579
slipping 76, 165, 198, 280, 283, 568, 582, 592
slips 10, 12, 13, 54, 80, 127, 150, 166, 184, 187, 213, 220, 347, 348, 361, 397, 399, 415, 430, 473, 488, 498, 527, 528, 552
slithered 589
slithering 565
slivered 239
slogging 562
slopes 81
sloppily 447
sloppiness 562
slops 420
sloshed 17, 18
sloshes 484
sloshing 290
slots 583
slower 74, 351
slowing 177, 359, 371, 485
slows 71, 96, 288, 486
slumbers 47
slumps 183, 253, 414
slurred 26
slush   color of 406
smacked 507
smacks 192, 564
smarter 121, 265, 383
smartest 100, 106, 172
smarts 608
smashes 101, 174, 390
smeared 557, 565
smearing 26
smears 334, 567
smeary 132
smelling 102, 223, 291, 558

smells   40, 73, 157, 184, 447, 514
smell's   589, 604
Smells   26, 536
smiled   246
smiles   7, 38, 43, 66, 76, 107, 133, 138, 202, 205, 207, 229, 266, 303, 306, 308, 367,
368, 384, 412, 419, 437, 533, 596, 598
smiles   tiniest of   435
smiling   33, 53, 62, 192, 193, 203, 238, 248, 278, 305, 336, 380, 456
smirking   26
smirks   303
smoldering   8, 84, 92, 118, 282, 304, 329
smoothed   460
smoothes   12
smoothing   9, 435
smoothly   46
smothered   47
smudged   439
snagging   101
snags   150, 392, 445
snails   579
snakelike   207
snakes   3, 22, 389, 402
snake's   192
Snakes   156
snapped   590
snapping   373
snaps   6, 42, 62, 176, 242, 250, 274, 351, 366, 386, 414, 455, 490, 537, 549, 605
snared   81
snares   48, 50, 52, 59, 60, 83, 87, 108, 141, 142, 166, 168, 200, 212, 293, 314, 384
snaring   469
Snarky   300
snarled   91
snarling   97, 226, 442
snarls   178, 254, 313, 526
snatched   468
snatches   550
sneaked   427
sneaks   293
sneering   398
sniffing   70, 176, 300, 354
sniffs   228
snipping   325
sniveling   23, 163
snore| 84
snoring   164, 205

snorting 355, 371

snouts 176

snow   smell of   249

snowbank 276

snowcapped 300

snowflakes 220, 580

snows 600

snow's   268, 369, 424, 472, 474, 483, 485, 486, 487, 492, 498, 554, 557, 561, 562, 565,
571, 573, 583, 584, 585, 589, 591, 592, 593, 596, 597, 598, 601, 604

Snow's   rest of   604

Snow's   scent of   597

Snow's   smell of   565

snowsuit 268

snuffling 176, 347

snuggled 418

snuggles 110, 482

snugly 349

snugness 445

So| 90

so|familiar 530

So|Peeta| 412

so|pure 310

so|you 309

So|you're 415

soaked   16, 92, 146, 153, 158, 173, 268, 393, 395, 535, 537, 546

soaking   54, 221, 249, 256, 355, 430, 456, 588, 593

soaks 287

soaps 41, 599

soars 267

sobbed 483

sobbing 258, 325, 342

sobered 162

sobers 221

sobs 15, 448, 488, 542, 606

socks 77, 109, 121, 128, 135, 148, 153, 154, 158, 167, 274, 287

sofas 239, 552

softens 63

softer 82

softly   54, 94, 123, 140, 158, 181, 187, 209, 270, 306, 308, 327, 342, 351, 365, 379,
392, 400, 467, 492, 523, 552, 588

soiled 205, 448

Soldier Everdeen   415, 432, 445, 526, 541, 550, 588

Soldier Gale Hawthorne   416

Soldier Hawthorne   464

Soldier Katniss Everdeen   416, 447, 547

Soldier Leeg 539
Soldier York 525, 526, 528
soldier title of 592
soldiers 231, 420, 437, 447, 452, 477, 495, 508, 511, 512, 518, 524, 531, 533, 534, 537, 538, 544, 555, 560, 572, 576, 582, 588, 589
soldier's 535
Soldiers 528
Soldiers Odair 534
soldiers sounds of 543
soles 333
solidly 86, 191
some|what 339
Somebody's 214
Somehow Haymitch 57
Somehow I'm 276, 312, 321, 328
Somehow Jackson 548
Somehow Rue 110
someone's 76, 84, 103, 169, 206, 368, 377, 403, 452, 532, 548, 549, 566, 567, 582
somersaults 215, 358
something|the 14
something's 112, 253, 351, 390, 485, 488, 564, 582
songbirds 246, 300, 369
songs 24, 124, 127, 315, 359, 467, 600
soothes 34
soothing 124, 184, 291, 376, 399, 408, 418, 479
soothingly 216
soreness 456, 518
sores 427, 492
sorts 155, 166, 235, 272, 347, 359, 386, 457, 490
souls 3
sounded 393, 511, 559, 562
soundlessly 75, 471
soundly 279
soundness 412
sounds 5, 24, 53, 70, 74, 84, 98, 114, 121, 166, 167, 168, 170, 176, 180, 215, 222, 249, 261, 285, 291, 300, 302, 303, 312, 322, 331, 335, 342, 374, 375, 376, 393, 422, 430, 444, 445, 446, 449, 468, 478, 481, 541, 545, 583
soundstage 439
soundtrack 191
soups 239
sources 59, 407
spaces 470, 476, 478, 484, 503, 587
spared 6, 395, 465, 586, 595
spares 432
sparkling 72, 94, 103, 114, 131, 371

sparkly		72, 412
spasms		352, 355, 473, 530
spawned		98, 239
speakers		183
speaks		71, 229, 240, 281, 315, 348, 358, 409, 429, 441, 472, 474, 481, 508, 519, 521, 530, 543, 549, 574, 589
speared		129, 270
spearheads		128
spearing		192, 357
spears		79, 167, 186, 293, 305, 314, 337
Special Defense		428, 436, 437, 444, 472, 484, 485, 493, 494, 499
Special Weaponry		437, 443, 460, 524, 590
specialists		498
specialized		271
specially		43, 512
specifically		76, 214, 216, 310, 383, 482, 594
specifics		496
specified		476
specifying		149
specks		476
speeches		236, 406, 439, 573
speeding		409
speeds		32, 150, 436, 533
spending		30, 216, 244, 250, 347, 479
spends		236, 299, 309, 315, 544, 579
spewing		102, 205, 301, 598
spews		337
spices		299
spied		110, 123
spies		509
spiked		22
spikes		72, 434, 517, 536
spiles	handful of	349
spilled		17
spilling		78, 218, 471, 472
spills		598
spins		220, 248, 445, 493, 506
spirits		26, 31, 43, 121, 146, 148, 239, 439, 528
spirits	bottle of	32
spits		239, 327
spitting		63, 525
splashes		181, 338
splashing		96, 106, 242, 350
splattered		490
splattering		80, 255, 317

splatters	177, 473
split pile of	466
splits	35, 55, 150
splotchy	57
spoiled	156, 200, 241, 267
spokes	335, 337, 339, 362
sponges	41
sponsors	26, 31, 32, 40, 57, 63, 68, 72, 73, 87, 88, 89, 90, 100, 107, 130, 157, 162, 185, 193, 381, 384
sponsor's	343
sponsorship	56
spontaneously	235, 331
spoonfuls	41, 57, 139, 161, 182
spotlessly	17
spotlights	513
spots	3, 266, 359, 370, 425, 449, 460, 465, 595
spotting	344
spouts	547
sprawled	205, 489
sprawling	540
sprawls	352
spraying	356
sprays	391, 582
spreading	80, 203, 271, 298, 334, 413, 449, 455, 483, 594
spreads	5, 104, 371, 380, 457, 495, 570
springs	201, 233, 345, 389, 498, 551
Spring's	603
springs lack of	349
sprinkled	115, 127, 239, 551
sprinting	370
sprints	121
sprouted	517
sprouting	261
sputtering	570
sputters	205
spying	114, 281
squads	531, 537
squad's	536
squares	345, 539
square's	9, 10, 245
squashing	477
squats	450
squatting	369, 386
squeaking	359, 487
squeaks	594

squeals 217
squeamishness 471
squeezed 94, 376
squeezes 174, 488
squeezing 597
squinting 224, 486
squints 31, 316, 541, 569
squirming 410
squirrels 28, 35, 48, 49, 59, 200, 300, 302, 430
squirrel's 347
stabbed 132, 177, 256, 361
stabbing 101, 358, 372, 491, 530
stabs 89, 351, 402
staged 140, 228, 332, 335, 577, 590
stages 85
staggered 363
staggering 14
stained 321
staining 581
stains 147, 339, 361, 546
staircases 232
stairways 411
stalked 56, 331
stalking 82
stalks 312
stalls 203
stammers 70
stamped 269, 344, 533, 540
stamps 362, 533
standards 433, 503, 507, 520
stands 47, 52, 53, 177, 200, 209, 219, 230, 247, 302, 316, 336, 367, 368, 390, 394, 396, 407, 417, 431, 533, 553, 567, 594
stanzas 586
Star Squad 537, 544, 564
stared 18
stares 53, 55, 224, 302, 321, 359, 499, 516, 523, 560, 570
staring 18, 29, 33, 46, 124, 127, 163, 183, 184, 207, 215, 228, 230, 240, 248, 280, 294, 308, 310, 327, 349, 371, 387, 472, 487, 508, 531, 551, 585, 588
stars 67, 103, 180, 199, 238, 239, 296, 363, 570
started 4, 12, 18, 29, 64, 81, 106, 144, 151, 156, 157, 203, 218, 224, 244, 246, 273, 281, 319, 343, 345, 363, 368, 379, 380, 448, 468, 517, 527, 530, 588, 591, 609
starters 78, 523, 543
starting 52, 56, 62, 71, 100, 140, 155, 211, 215, 258, 302, 315, 330, 342, 370, 371, 372, 375, 382, 392, 420, 466, 472, 476, 485, 495, 507, 512, 555
startled 81, 82, 157, 188, 236, 309, 451, 459

startles   144, 196, 351

starts   14, 31, 41, 42, 55, 58, 75, 85, 103, 147, 175, 191, 204, 220, 236, 242, 244, 249, 283, 298, 302, 318, 327, 338, 343, 367, 368, 370, 372, 375, 386, 406, 437, 464, 466, 531, 554, 555, 563, 566, 579

starvation   brink of   272

Starvation's   16

starved   262, 324, 482, 520

starves   394

starving   8, 16, 41, 56, 58, 159, 160, 185, 205, 258, 267, 271, 284, 306, 342, 404, 456, 507, 528

stashed   254

stashes   414

staticfilled   232

stationed   232

stations   51, 54, 485

stations   list of   314

statues   178

stayed   56, 95, 100, 132, 192, 247, 413, 474, 495, 564

staying   20, 57, 76, 81, 124, 165, 282, 297, 301, 343, 345, 416, 505, 537, 571, 576

steadied   61

steadily   15, 171, 279, 321

steadiness   220, 504

steadying   269, 397

steaks   143

Stealing Gale   499

stealing's   60

stealthily   346

steaming   47, 214, 223, 270, 298, 351, 413, 484

steaming   smell of   268

steeper   582

steering   352

stemmed   41, 240, 486

stems   27

stenciled   34

stenciling   64

Stephanie Nooney   608

stepped   14, 71, 206, 218, 246, 256, 300, 310, 433, 488

stepping   25, 67, 245, 261

steps   10, 12, 13, 15, 51, 67, 78, 106, 116, 118, 126, 184, 190, 230, 231, 235, 236, 240, 242, 246, 248, 253, 255, 276, 287, 289, 290, 293, 301, 334, 340, 363, 372, 391, 397, 408, 411, 426, 503, 512, 513, 514, 521, 524, 533, 546, 551, 558, 563, 570, 572, 573, 594, 595, 603

sternly   216

stew's   61

sticking   83, 419, 541, 548, 591

sticks   168, 203, 209, 216, 369, 417, 429, 528, 602

stiffening   102
stiffly   43, 206, 255, 278
stiffness   104, 181, 199
stifles   94
still|and   373
Still|I   321
stilled   489
stiller   76
stingers   101, 102, 107, 110, 114, 132, 134
stinging   91, 94, 217, 303, 373, 583
stings   34, 91, 99, 102, 103, 104, 105, 106, 109, 114, 122, 134, 140, 195, 300, 421, 430
Stitched   326
stitches   291, 419, 519, 521, 570
stockades   265
stocked   113, 300, 592
stockpiled   519
stockpiling   203
stoically   606
stomach.| 163
stomach| 219
stomachs   6, 8, 25, 107, 136, 158, 165, 388, 574
stomach's   122
stomp   62, 360
stomping   167, 190
stomps   526
stonecutters   504
stones   119, 141, 149, 226, 253, 405, 501, 503, 546, 547, 548, 551, 555, 576
stone's   84, 201
stops   33, 57, 68, 71, 88, 102, 107, 116, 118, 160, 164, 183, 187, 196, 205, 224, 281,
282, 307, 316, 327, 333, 350, 351, 352, 360, 369, 397, 447, 450, 475, 484, 523, 530, 546
stored   609
storefront   568
storefronts   228
stories   204, 490, 492
storming   508
storms   10
stoutly   352
stowed   201
stowing   602
Straaten   608
straddling   86
stragglers   404, 584
Straggling   16
straighter   238
strains   127, 129, 331, 348

stranded	337, 542
strands	65, 94, 140, 203, 216, 219, 318, 342
strangely	171, 342
strangers	192, 197, 242, 476, 498, 511, 562, 601
strangest	569
strangled	12, 261, 502, 582
straps	80, 81, 150, 443
strategically	99, 199, 306
strategies	40, 41
strawberries	6, 7, 8, 9, 13, 28, 29, 259
strayed	59
streaked	111, 225, 308
streaks	101, 140, 311
streams	36, 82, 156, 239, 300, 349, 397, 475, 511
streetful	548
streets	3, 10, 16, 32, 36, 37, 75, 193, 196, 201, 243, 246, 250, 265, 266, 267, 268, 272, 311, 332, 511, 538, 548, 550, 559, 563, 567, 569, 575, 576, 581, 598
street's	451
strengthened	261
strengthening	525
strengths	50
stresses	478
stretched	140, 141, 208, 227, 337, 563
stretchers	447
stretches	300, 441, 560
stretching	104, 551, 586
strewn	78, 388, 486, 552
strides	426, 447
strikes	10, 159, 233, 326, 350, 366, 384, 386, 393, 394, 444, 521
strings	162, 584
string's	55
stripes	569, 579
stripped	33, 279, 290, 431, 433, 456, 494, 536, 596, 599
stripping	309, 315
strips	82, 108, 335, 369, 371, 558
strokes	154, 257, 281, 338, 356, 359, 383, 480, 518
stroking	56, 89, 140, 258, 365, 408
strolling	110, 117, 273, 540
strolls	475
stronger	83, 97, 137, 154, 208, 301, 342, 457, 600
strongest	257, 287, 288, 394, 427
strongholds	272
strongly	72, 125, 456, 541
structures	137
struggled	40, 176

struggles		232, 354, 367, 396, 449
struggling		12, 41, 59, 75, 102, 139, 151, 183, 315, 375, 517, 566, 584, 590, 607
stubble	outline of	259
stubs	216	
studded		308, 334, 433
students		52
studiously		296
studying		264, 414, 436, 439, 442, 527, 562
stuffs	107, 232, 278, 365, 431	
stuff's	203	
stumbled		90, 142
stumbles		302
stumbling		16, 89, 175, 353, 362, 510
stumps		466
stunned		12, 76, 151, 159, 191, 329, 341, 545, 576, 598
stupidly		42
sturdily		81, 162
styled	216, 414, 433	
stylists	32, 34, 35, 41, 42, 48, 51, 57, 66, 67, 71, 207, 235, 308, 569, 594	
stylist's		309
Stylists		531
subduing		288
subjecting		496
subjects		471
submerges		337
subsided		119, 402
substances		301
Subterfuges		398
subtly	121	
succeeded		239, 541
successfully		40, 608
sucked		236, 354, 366, 406
Suddenly I'm		49, 72
Suddenly Wiress		368
suffered		308, 316, 431, 456
suffocated		593
suffocating		200
sugarcoating		528
suggested		189, 321, 402, 413, 435, 456, 496
suggesting		19, 49, 77, 212, 362, 384, 439, 441, 442, 449, 508, 509, 519
suggests		36, 52, 65, 104, 208, 237, 281, 284, 374, 385, 412, 430, 438, 500, 508, 510, 573
suits	7, 273, 438, 456, 486, 521	
sullenly		434
summer's		67, 403

sunbeams		94
sunburned		433
Sunday		59, 204, 210, 211, 212, 245, 294
Sundays		200, 202, 210, 215, 293
sun's		79, 90, 106, 146, 339, 349, 580
sunsets		325
sunsoftened		369
supplements		387
supplied		200
supplier		465
supplies		78, 84, 85, 86, 92, 96, 108, 110, 112, 114, 115, 116, 117, 119, 120, 123, 126, 127, 128, 152, 163, 171, 179, 192, 206, 262, 300, 336, 410, 421, 445, 447, 476, 508, 519, 555, 568, 570, 571, 574
supplies	circle of	116
supplies	layout of	115
Supply Station		476
supported		228, 472, 478
supports		99, 191, 571
supposedly		54, 219, 531
suppressed		538
suppressing		58, 310, 546
surfaced		567
surfaces		356, 384, 441, 443, 483, 607
surfacing		365
surgeons		344
surges	584	
surgically		34, 187, 206, 461
surging		392, 400
surprise	element of	591
surprise	flicker of	277
surprised		20, 31, 73, 85, 165, 235, 270, 284, 321, 384, 441, 492, 505, 576, 588, 591, 602
surprises		21, 453
surprisingly		14, 58, 159, 167, 247, 343, 347
surreal	106, 165, 411	
surrounded		9, 128, 194, 207, 317, 334, 445, 485
surrounds		174, 200, 325, 352, 354
surveys		151
survival	secret of	67
survived		72, 83, 104, 119, 132, 145, 177, 288, 354, 398, 407, 416, 427, 440, 487, 500, 513, 556, 567
survives		582
surviving		11, 110, 120, 178, 399
survivors		404, 454, 457, 512, 574
suspected		39, 272, 335, 398, 596

suspects   list of   276
suspended   116, 325, 360, 455
suspicions   57, 90, 315, 345, 454, 463
suspiciously   48, 424
sustainable   596
sustained   171, 396
sustaining   79
sustaining   importance of   149
sutures   570
Suzanne   609
Suzanne Collins   1, 198, 401, 609
Suzanne Murphy   608
swallowed   10, 294, 549, 570
swallowing   249, 346, 371
swallows   92, 139, 146, 470
swamped   446
swapped   6
swarming   22
swathed   220, 593
swaying   98, 345
swearing   97
swears   453
sweat   sheen of   139, 345, 501
sweating   68, 147, 261, 294, 314
sweetly   34, 459, 467
sweetness   104, 298, 434
sweets   239, 277, 278
sweetshop   253, 287
swelled   18, 257
swells   174, 386
swerves   453
swiftly   18, 54, 179, 241, 325, 383, 388, 562
swimmer   336, 378
swimmers   337
swims   370, 392
swinging   181, 540, 557
swings   32, 341, 426, 476, 502, 583
swipes   390, 484
swiping   153
swirling   52, 91, 359
swirls   94, 315, 582
switchblades   357
switching   228
swooping   118
swoops   62

swords	293, 337
sympathies	157, 590
symptoms	82, 526
syringes	396
systems	486, 508
tables	111, 239, 240, 316
table's	364
Tables	239
tabletop	35
tablets	601
tabs	10
Tacked	499
tackles	547
tagged	504
tailbone	277, 278, 279, 280
tailbone's	279
taillights	221
tainted	154, 281
takers	16, 242, 506

takes 6, 15, 23, 26, 32, 35, 45, 48, 56, 62, 63, 66, 73, 74, 83, 86, 88, 89, 93, 97, 101, 105, 108, 119, 120, 122, 134, 135, 138, 146, 163, 167, 169, 176, 177, 178, 180, 181, 192, 193, 195, 197, 199, 202, 208, 209, 224, 225, 228, 238, 252, 255, 256, 257, 264, 266, 268, 275, 281, 286, 289, 290, 292, 293, 294, 302, 303, 306, 314, 315, 325, 330, 333, 334, 335, 339, 347, 351, 356, 357, 363, 364, 367, 370, 376, 377, 380, 384, 389, 390, 392, 399, 400, 407, 409, 413, 414, 421, 428, 430, 434, 436, 437, 441, 442, 446, 450, 451, 453, 457, 466, 481, 482, 484, 488, 489, 490, 491, 493, 495, 507, 514, 518, 524, 527, 529, 536, 538, 540, 547, 559, 569, 581, 586, 593, 594, 603, 604, 605

Taking Rue		108
taking	chance of	460
taking	idea of	271
taking	satisfaction of	579
talents	58, 315, 320, 331	
talked	60, 72, 148, 211, 235, 275, 295, 413, 490, 522, 573	
talker	435	

talking 6, 40, 44, 48, 50, 53, 61, 65, 72, 87, 115, 151, 157, 159, 186, 188, 189, 194, 197, 213, 216, 225, 241, 244, 278, 285, 294, 305, 309, 311, 312, 315, 327, 333, 363, 373, 380, 398, 406, 409, 411, 425, 459, 462, 466, 468, 470, 472, 481, 510, 515, 523, 544, 574, 588, 601

talks	315, 317, 431, 527
taller	208
tallying	423, 572
talons	223, 395
tampered	497
tangles	339
tangling	62
taped	44, 462, 517, 539

tapered 256, 348, 349

tapes 296, 297, 298, 523, 548

tapestries 588

taping 439, 462, 469, 491, 548

tapped 173, 264

targeted 101, 340, 452, 596

targeting 357, 452

targets 32, 318, 352, 382, 452, 496, 532, 533, 537, 556, 576, 581

tarlike 548

tartness 5

tasks 127

tassels 572

tasted 30, 166, 387

tastes 30, 127, 164, 290, 435, 555

tastier 6

tasting 176, 239, 240, 543

tattooed 239, 447, 569

tattoos 33, 216, 283, 325, 410, 426, 434

taunting 14, 477

teachers 217, 285

teaches 293

teamed 152, 389

teaming 86, 139, 162

teammates 303, 325

teams 37, 39, 40, 190, 235, 243, 272, 605

team's 74, 223, 428, 429, 455, 495

teardrop 551

tea's 271

teased 317, 319

teasing 194, 203, 310, 507

teasingly 97, 151

tech 100, 268, 411, 438, 472

technically 51, 73, 108, 129, 306, 398

techniques 51, 298, 519

techno 493

technological 505

teenagers 584

teetering 102, 116, 117

televised 10, 11, 26, 57, 61, 83, 217, 324, 433, 478, 538, 549, 601

television|what 285

televisions 116, 404, 481

television's 245

tells 10, 23, 67, 191, 219, 226, 237, 257, 270, 273, 281, 314, 323, 333, 334, 356, 365, 367, 371, 388, 397, 431, 432, 438, 446, 448, 454, 457, 461, 463, 471, 475, 480, 483, 485, 491, 505, 507, 510, 518, 523, 524, 526, 528, 529, 532, 533, 537, 540, 552, 559, 560, 564, 567, 571,

575, 576, 587, 588, 597, 603, 605

temperatures 577
temples 67, 291
Templesmith 457
temporarily 50, 101, 353, 372, 482
temptations 240
tempted 40, 43, 48, 132, 424
tended 310, 589
tending 263
tendrils 351, 352
tenements 270
tenses 571
tentatively 106, 108, 118, 184, 391, 501
tents 538, 542
terminated 433
terrified 15, 19, 47, 58, 119, 179, 262, 334, 404, 518, 536, 582
terrifying 174, 193, 203, 306, 583
terror expression of 42
terrorized 261
tesserae 8, 9, 12, 16, 19, 28, 202, 267
tested 474, 526
testing 219, 348, 356, 436
tests 586
tethered 139, 168, 601
thanked 18, 211, 230
thankfully 163, 304
thanking 193, 478
That'd 202, 537
that'll 161, 524, 541
that's 3, 5, 7, 8, 12, 13, 18, 21, 22, 23, 31, 38, 39, 40, 42, 43, 45, 48, 49, 56, 57, 58, 59, 61, 62, 65, 75, 76, 78, 79, 80, 82, 83, 84, 85, 86, 99, 100, 105, 107, 110, 111, 112, 113, 116, 117, 122, 123, 127, 132, 134, 135, 136, 137, 138, 139, 140, 141, 144, 145, 146, 147, 151, 153, 155, 157, 158, 159, 160, 161, 163, 164, 167, 168, 170, 172, 173, 174, 176, 186, 188, 190, 191, 192, 194, 203, 207, 208, 212, 213, 220, 222, 227, 228, 230, 232, 234, 235, 236, 238, 240, 242, 244, 248, 249, 251, 254, 257, 259, 263, 265, 268, 269, 270, 271, 273, 275, 276, 281, 283, 285, 286, 288, 289, 291, 292, 296, 298, 299, 301, 302, 306, 309, 312, 313, 315, 316, 319, 320, 322, 323, 327, 328, 329, 332, 333, 334, 335, 336, 341, 343, 344, 347, 352, 355, 360, 363, 364, 365, 367, 369, 370, 371, 373, 375, 376, 377, 378, 379, 380, 381, 383, 384, 387, 394, 397, 400, 402, 404, 405, 408, 410, 411, 412, 413, 414, 415, 418, 419, 423, 426, 429, 430, 432, 435, 439, 441, 442, 443, 445, 448, 449, 450, 452, 453, 455, 456, 458, 460, 465, 466, 468, 469, 471, 472, 473, 478, 480, 482, 484, 487, 488, 489, 491, 492, 494, 495, 496, 497, 498, 500, 501, 502, 504, 507, 508, 509, 513, 515, 516, 518, 519, 520, 523, 524, 525, 526, 527, 528, 530, 532, 535, 536, 541, 543, 549, 551, 553, 554, 555, 557, 560, 561, 562, 563, 564, 565, 566, 567, 572, 573, 575, 581, 583, 584, 585, 587, 589, 593, 596, 599, 608
That's Beetee 363

That's Rue's 174

thawing 247

the| 394

them|notify 456

themselves| 117

then| 135, 155, 221

then|and 221

then|for 523

then|I 165

then|if 274

then|I'm 509

then|what 165

theoretically 379, 562, 581

there'd 280, 398, 424

there'll 20, 22, 49

there's 2, 3, 6, 9, 11, 12, 13, 16, 20, 21, 22, 24, 25, 26, 30, 34, 41, 44, 45, 49, 52, 53, 54, 55, 61, 62, 63, 65, 67, 70, 71, 75, 77, 79, 81, 83, 84, 85, 86, 88, 89, 90, 91, 92, 93, 97, 98, 99, 101, 106, 109, 111, 112, 115, 117, 119, 120, 121, 122, 123, 124, 125, 126, 127, 130, 131, 132, 133, 135, 137, 139, 140, 143, 145, 146, 147, 149, 152, 154, 156, 157, 159, 160, 162, 164, 165, 167, 170, 172, 173, 174, 176, 178, 179, 180, 181, 183, 185, 186, 190, 191, 192, 193, 194, 196, 200, 203, 205, 208, 209, 214, 215, 216, 221, 222, 223, 225, 228, 229, 230, 232, 236, 239, 243, 245, 247, 250, 251, 252, 253, 255, 258, 259, 261, 264, 266, 267, 269, 270, 274, 276, 277, 280, 283, 285, 286, 288, 290, 291, 294, 296, 298, 299, 300, 301, 304, 308, 310, 311, 312, 314, 319, 321, 322, 323, 325, 326, 327, 328, 330, 331, 332, 335, 336, 337, 338, 340, 341, 342, 343, 344, 345, 346, 347, 349, 350, 351, 354, 355, 356, 361, 364, 365, 366, 367, 368, 369, 370, 371, 372, 374, 377, 378, 379, 380, 382, 383, 384, 385, 386, 387, 388, 389, 390, 391, 392, 393, 395, 396, 399, 402, 403, 404, 406, 408, 409, 410, 415, 417, 425, 427, 431, 435, 436, 438, 439, 440, 442, 443, 444, 445, 446, 447, 449, 451, 452, 453, 454, 456, 458, 459, 463, 470, 471, 472, 475, 476, 478, 479, 480, 481, 484, 487, 488, 489, 492, 494, 497, 498, 501, 508, 511, 513, 515, 516, 520, 522, 524, 525, 527, 529, 532, 533, 534, 536, 537, 539, 540, 541, 547, 548, 550, 552, 554, 555, 557, 558, 560, 561, 562, 563, 564, 566, 567, 568, 569, 570, 571, 572, 573, 574, 575, 577, 580, 582, 584, 586, 587, 589, 590, 591, 592, 593, 594, 595, 598, 599, 600, 603, 606

There's Peeta 218, 592

they| 375

they|remake 431

they'll 25, 37, 49, 56, 57, 58, 73, 81, 82, 89, 90, 102, 109, 120, 123, 125, 126, 132, 141, 148, 155, 162, 164, 172, 209, 221, 233, 250, 274, 285, 298, 300, 303, 337, 338, 344, 383, 385, 396, 397, 399, 406, 411, 416, 419, 421, 423, 429, 439, 475, 477, 481, 483, 489, 495, 510, 546, 556, 557, 562, 567, 580, 583

thickens 328

thicker 354, 551

thighs 62, 77, 184, 403

thing's 36, 63, 115, 531

think| 151

think|this 304

think|those	177
think|you	572
thinking|it's	322
thinking|you	518
thinning	30, 356
thirds	378, 551
thirstily	154, 291
thirsting	388
thirsty|	83
Thirteen|	473
Thirteen|dead	473
Thirteen's	273, 484, 487
thirties	447
this|this	86
Thom	256, 257, 605
thorns	284
thoroughly	196, 218
those|cousins	208
though|and	165
thought|and	116
thought|I'll	505
thought|they've	515
thoughtfully	110, 144
thousands	12, 230, 272, 384, 407, 431, 450, 515, 519, 545
thrashes	408
threads	133, 392
Thread's	256, 265, 285, 405
threatened	247, 262, 409, 516
threatening	136, 138, 435, 497, 511, 583
threatens	9, 92, 189, 262, 405
threats	208, 492, 589
three|I'm	147
Thresh|and	515
Thresh's	152, 153, 163, 229, 230, 232, 233
thrilled	29, 186, 330, 346, 572
thriving	274, 282
throated	409
throats	357
throbbing	100, 291
throbs	89, 260, 391
throwbacks	327
throwers	315
throwing	14, 18, 31, 52, 53, 186, 203, 208, 238, 244, 245, 250, 251, 288, 293, 465, 493, 535
throwing idea of	240

throws   38, 44, 54, 113, 116, 119, 150, 251, 278, 302, 308, 318, 325, 358, 370, 377, 386, 421, 452, 469, 473, 530, 538, 567, 571, 603

thrusts   115, 181

thumbs   38, 70, 149, 487

thunder's   158

thwarting   266

tickling   38, 507

ticks   57

tidbits   320

ties   371, 373, 411

tightening   161

tightens   32, 124, 157, 202, 279, 286, 488

tighter   10, 18, 55

tightly   10, 18, 25, 39, 103, 178, 179, 180, 183, 197, 198, 201, 211, 212, 229, 246, 266, 298, 301, 347, 350, 351, 359, 388, 391, 392, 400, 411, 419, 425, 470, 484, 511, 529, 536, 538, 569

Tigris   569, 570, 573, 574, 576, 577, 579, 580

Tigrises   573

Tigris's   569, 573, 575, 577, 578, 583

tiled   74, 228, 239, 418, 427, 473, 523, 563, 582

tiles   75, 473, 557, 582, 593

tiles| 428

tilted   53, 341, 563

tilting   58, 151, 391

tilts   50, 223, 249, 394, 438, 560

Tim O'Brien   608, 609

time   nick of   118

time   passage of   180

time|there   195

timed   361

times   8, 18, 19, 20, 21, 32, 40, 49, 53, 91, 102, 114, 118, 124, 129, 132, 144, 158, 164, 179, 202, 211, 216, 220, 225, 232, 238, 244, 256, 257, 258, 268, 273, 275, 303, 321, 327, 353, 378, 380, 383, 407, 410, 422, 435, 450, 467, 482, 484, 498, 504, 507, 517, 539, 574, 580, 582, 583, 589, 595, 605

tinctures   256

tinged   345, 586

tingling   33, 604

tiniest   69, 422

tinkles   325

tins   211

tinted   53, 263, 516

tiny   whir of   436

tipped   86, 101, 453, 521, 565

tipping   157, 253, 289, 398

tips   24, 26, 65, 71, 306, 318, 380, 582, 586

tiptoes	116
tirades	157
tiredly	54, 275, 415
tiredness	89
Title Master	608
Title Page Table	610
Titus	76
to|	566
to|sell	491
to|to	75, 125
toasting	248, 327, 330
toasty	139
tock	363, 364, 365, 366, 375, 493, 531
tocking	366, 368
today's	172, 199
Toddlers	584
toes	28, 53, 59, 201, 208, 215, 219, 274, 545, 607
toilets	240
tolerated	540, 592
tolerating	214
tolled	365
tolling	350, 366
tomatoes	42
Tomorrow I'll	91, 127
Tomorrow's	156
tones	24, 88, 133
tongues	65, 310, 312, 346, 350
tonight's	5, 473
tons	510
too|	578
tools	267, 434
topics	4, 368
topped	3, 164, 227, 429
torches	22, 37, 83, 85, 98, 100, 266
torchlight	109
tormented	554
torture agony of	412
tortured	267, 288, 405, 417, 470, 481, 482, 495, 517, 523, 535, 545, 554, 562, 565, 604
torturers	310, 463
tortures	394
torturing	335, 375, 376
torturous	11, 354
tossed	22, 219, 292, 340, 370, 522
tosses	5, 166, 206, 235, 248, 278, 292, 306, 309, 327, 339, 351, 363, 528

tossing   31, 72, 141, 219, 261, 321, 345, 369, 386, 418, 577
total   disorientation of   478
touches   14, 188, 228, 281, 305, 326, 411, 419, 435, 457, 521, 595
toughened   586
towels   548
towers   386
towing   338, 372
toys   471
traces   151, 557, 602
tracked   91, 292, 561
tracker   76, 98, 99, 101, 102, 104, 105, 106, 109, 110, 112, 113, 114, 115, 123,
132, 134, 135, 136, 173, 174, 192, 275, 333, 398, 422, 429, 434, 443, 496, 498, 512, 523, 547,
551, 560, 565, 593
trackers   430
tracker's   76
tracking   76, 78, 82, 87, 90, 106, 131, 132, 206, 210, 458, 562, 589
tracks   121, 132, 166, 268, 273, 279, 372, 512, 516, 519, 548, 551, 559
Tracy   608
traded   29, 424
trademarks   609
traders   90, 271
trades   4, 49, 196, 202, 369
trading   20, 59, 202, 266, 507, 577
traditionally   51, 110, 202, 313
trailed   434
trailing   279, 411, 569
trails   13, 82, 118, 134, 153, 155, 316, 330, 348
trained   14, 18, 20, 22, 36, 37, 51, 63, 137, 140, 172, 188, 230, 294, 384, 405, 410, 452,
524, 552
trainers   53
Training Center   37, 39, 40, 44, 50, 51, 57, 66, 71, 88, 117, 127, 184, 186, 193,
237, 285, 302, 308, 312, 315, 331, 336, 341, 342, 393, 396, 545, 598, 599
trains   6, 224, 445, 512, 514, 538, 559
train's   196, 220
trains   pair of   514
trains| 561
traitors   45
trampled   357, 374
transferable   609
transferred   549
transfers   249
transfixed   581
transformed   60, 77, 91, 100, 238, 265, 347, 402, 585, 593
transforming   196, 297, 304, 354, 356
transforms   297, 521

translates		519, 550
transmits		425
transmitted		24, 609
transporting		23, 503
trapdoor		232, 485

trapped   32, 81, 99, 114, 115, 132, 150, 152, 173, 182, 188, 277, 287, 338, 345, 376, 399, 413, 509, 510, 511, 516, 538, 547, 556, 571, 577, 586, 593

trapping		50, 120, 454, 499
traveling		106, 122, 600
travels		93, 571
trays		23, 421, 529, 530
treads		77, 558
Treason	Treaty of	10
treasures		584
treated		20, 24, 100, 109, 235, 262, 334, 423, 427, 430, 447, 498, 530
treating		95, 134, 135, 364, 542, 604
treats		258, 291, 293

trees   3, 24, 28, 44, 74, 78, 80, 82, 88, 91, 93, 102, 103, 105, 107, 109, 110, 114, 118, 119, 121, 123, 127, 128, 149, 150, 151, 153, 158, 174, 175, 184, 224, 227, 230, 245, 268, 275, 276, 293, 309, 311, 339, 341, 346, 349, 357, 358, 362, 364, 374, 384, 385, 388, 397, 418, 436, 466, 467, 468, 475, 485, 503

tree's		386
Trees		103, 394, 560
trees	availability of	75
trees	clump of	85
trekking		81
trembling		87, 91, 92, 168, 290, 313, 359, 376, 391, 434, 583, 604
tremors		600
trends	216	
trespassed		589
trespassing		3, 276
tresses	83, 433	
trial's	601	

tributes   11, 19, 22, 23, 31, 32, 35, 36, 37, 38, 39, 40, 44, 48, 50, 51, 53, 54, 56, 61, 66, 67, 70, 71, 73, 76, 79, 80, 82, 83, 86, 90, 91, 94, 104, 110, 111, 114, 116, 119, 120, 129, 130, 141, 149, 162, 172, 173, 177, 186, 190, 191, 192, 203, 207, 217, 222, 228, 229, 237, 242, 286, 287, 288, 293, 296, 299, 300, 301, 302, 305, 308, 309, 312, 313, 314, 315, 317, 318, 319, 320, 323, 327, 332, 334, 335, 338, 346, 348, 369, 370, 373, 374, 376, 382, 384, 385, 394, 397, 399, 413, 423, 429, 430, 432, 435, 446, 460, 555, 565, 607

tribute's		13, 92
Tributes		1, 2, 333, 531, 610
tributes	circle of	335
tributes	ring of	78
tributes|		74
tricked		561

tricking		154
trickles		358, 486
trickling		415
tricks	28, 122, 346, 354	
tridents		314, 337, 339, 340, 353, 370
tries	11, 67, 69, 76, 97, 121, 137, 147, 257, 270, 278, 293, 309, 328, 338, 358, 367, 368, 405, 445, 452, 472, 475, 482, 496, 501, 502, 511, 527, 560, 586, 593	
triggered		61, 357, 365, 513, 550
triggering		224, 498, 546, 551, 576
triggers		93, 200, 434, 531, 548
trills	13, 174, 243, 275	
trimmed		316
trio's	362	
tripled	90	
tripped		26, 58, 241
trips	221, 254, 469, 514, 518	
triumphantly		14
tromp	363	
tromping		122
troops	446, 503, 519, 532, 587	
trophies		561
trots	11	
troubles		125, 158, 281, 288, 300, 470
troubling		265, 468
trucks	235, 559	
trudges		265, 559
true|could		160
trumpets		129, 144, 182, 189, 302
trunk's	388	
trusted		60, 211, 400, 414, 433, 518, 569, 572
trusts	196	
trying	idea of	505
trying	stress of	162
tubers	28, 215	
tubes	183, 184, 185, 395, 396, 399, 559	
tub's	594	
tucked	9, 254, 290, 418	
tuckered		289
tucking		104, 154, 160
tucks	38, 248, 280, 498	
tufts	346	
tugging		394
tugs	283, 339, 457	
tuned	67, 286, 463, 491	
tunes	600	

tunics   37, 42
tunnels   32, 200, 445, 532, 538, 557, 559, 560, 561
turkeys   60, 430
turnips   420, 424, 528
TV   29, 447, 555
twelve age of   8, 262
Twelve   mayor of   605
Twelve   remainder of 423
Twelve|if I'd   438
twenties   203, 434, 537
twenty reality of   47
twigs   245
Twill's   270, 273
twinkles   44
twins   47, 299
twirling   73, 326, 521
twisted   77, 143, 259, 268, 270, 273, 443, 466, 469, 489, 504, 595
twisting   101, 179, 232, 345, 390, 477, 557, 591
twists   205, 271, 312, 352, 437, 446
twitches   176, 408, 560
twitching   62, 102, 352, 354, 358
twitchy   328
types   53, 283
typing   547
ublished   609
ugliest   2, 407
Uh   58, 432
um| 13
Um|all   69
Um|very   497
unacceptable   470, 499
unanswered   113, 238
unanticipated   277
unattainably   56
unattractive   35
unauthorized   525, 572, 587
unbelievably   211, 564
unblemished   511
unblinkingly   127
unbolts   579
unceremoniously   408
uncertainly   108, 442
unchanged   67, 140, 216, 261, 398, 503, 594
uncharacteristic   415
unchecked   140, 271

uncomplaining	134
uncomplicated	212
uncomprehendingly	103, 183, 397, 416, 515
unconditionally	504
unconsciousness	180, 585
uncontrollably	352, 353
unconvinced	278, 543
unconvincing	70
uncooperative	118
undefeated	151
undependable	230
underarms	33
underdressed	577
underestimates	454
underfed	31, 52, 171
undergarments	77, 290, 333, 354, 364, 365, 568
Underland Chronicles	609
undermined	207
undermining	335
underscored	472
undershirts	361
understands	249, 403, 537, 597
understatement	118
undertaken	450
undetectable	121, 147
Undisciplined	525
undisturbed	121, 131
undoubtedly	29, 121, 303, 320
undrinkable	340
undulating	334
unease	42, 114, 542
uneasiness	248
unendurable	482
unexpectedly	26, 113, 404, 532
unexplained	256
unfairness	251
unfazed	314
unfocused	472
unforeseen	459
unforgivable	147
unforgiving	192, 308
unfortunately	17, 27, 41, 150, 208, 282, 306, 379, 408, 441, 516
unhappily	12, 245, 312, 485
unharmed	209, 329, 415, 451
unhinged	171, 335

unhooks	518
uniforms	231, 265, 269, 272, 425, 531, 538, 554, 564, 568, 579, 581, 585, 596, 598
unifying	524
unimportant	533, 544
unimpressed	422
uninjured	81, 494
uninspiring	544
uninvited	207
unitard	36, 46
units	422
unlatches	527
unleashed	561
unleashes	544
Unless Tigris	570
Unless|unless|	210
Unlike Gale	202
unlit	123, 128
unlivable	260, 410
unloading	469
unlocked	74
unlocks	550, 604
unmarried	222
unmistakably	133, 176, 226
unnaturally	138
unnerving	265, 468
unnoticed	85, 213, 230, 271, 383, 570
unobserved	98, 466
unprotected	398
unquenchable	585
unrattled	454
unraveled	190
unraveling	432
unravels	371, 581
unreachable	5, 47, 284, 342, 374
unrealistic	442
unrecognizable	102, 203, 216
unresisting	368, 560
unresponsive	341
unrolls	388
unscripted	441, 465
unsmiling	586
unspecified	483
unsteadily	431
unsuccessfully	309, 547
untangling	41, 106

untested 448

unties 348

until|until 570

untucked 12, 585

unveils 453

unwanted 4, 120

unwashed stink of 426

unwinding 388

unwittingly 275

unzipping 180

unzips 179, 309, 326, 342

updated 284, 444

updates 90, 482, 498, 504, 519, 579

upgrades 268

upholstered 412

uprisings 209, 212, 213, 284, 324, 459

uprisings verge of 213

uprooted 33

ups 43, 235, 298, 545

upscale 227

upset| 414

upsets 155

upstaged 55

urgently 412

urges 195

urging 148

usefulness 112, 481, 591

useless concept of 421

ushered 206, 294

ushers 484, 496

using 60, 121, 153, 177, 212, 244, 247, 256, 273, 285, 301, 302, 315, 320, 438, 440, 459, 462, 486, 487, 508, 584, 587, 590, 591, 597

using necessity of 601

uttered 534

utterly 38, 73, 125, 172, 424, 495, 563

vacuumed 354

vaguely 17, 68, 153, 207, 212, 241, 291, 316, 348, 354, 427, 474, 588

validation 235

Valleys 81

vanished 45, 56, 102, 126, 185, 222, 359, 367, 566

vanishes 87, 100, 283, 374, 447, 547, 582, 584

vanishing 103, 153

vapor body of 351

vaporized 13

variables 56

variations   508
varying   397
vases   194, 232
vastly   388, 432
vastness   227
veered   213
veers   178
vegetables   17, 239, 295, 304, 420
vehicles   437, 563, 581
veins   104, 127, 390, 396, 485, 495, 516, 586
Venia   33, 34, 64, 186, 187, 190, 216, 217, 223, 240, 282, 283, 303, 325, 427, 431, 434, 439, 594
Venia's   216, 326, 426, 427, 429
vents   508
ventures   97
verandah   228, 229, 231, 232
verging   92
verses   24
versions   149, 226, 304, 499
very| 316
vetoes   520
vials   259
vibrating   118, 316, 331
viciously   23
Vick   202, 241, 247, 262, 376
victims   16, 84, 300, 461, 565, 581, 590, 596
victories   415
victors   11, 155, 161, 182, 188, 191, 207, 211, 214, 220, 222, 228, 236, 248, 287, 288, 292, 293, 296, 297, 298, 303, 305, 307, 309, 310, 311, 314, 316, 317, 318, 319, 327, 328, 330, 331, 332, 336, 339, 348, 373, 395, 417, 432, 433, 435, 456, 493, 526, 535, 540, 577, 596, 597
victor's   128, 191, 222, 254
Victors   222, 288, 293, 598
Victor's Village   161, 165, 199, 201, 204, 211, 252, 264, 265, 287, 402, 406, 408, 470, 471, 602
victors field of   395
Victory Banquet   193
Victory Tour   199, 202, 217, 222, 232, 244, 268, 272, 283, 293, 403, 409, 483, 503, 512, 513, 520
Victory Tours   207
victory   trumpets of   180
viewed   35, 82, 190, 207, 208, 402, 428, 433, 474, 484
viewers   56, 71, 90, 379
views   527
villages   502, 504
vines   52, 137, 139, 325, 339, 341, 352, 353, 354, 357, 359, 364, 371, 373, 382, 390,

391, 447, 569

vines   tangle of   351

violates   202

vipers   93

viruses   492

vises   427

visibly   486

visions   496

visited   503

visiting   456

visitors   226, 586

visits   214, 216, 588, 603

voices   61, 85, 86, 96, 112, 174, 253, 297, 331, 379, 396, 399, 449, 467, 489, 539, 581

voices| 377

voicing   241, 556

Volts   317, 318, 363, 365, 367, 368, 389

volumes   521

voluntarily   558, 560, 577

volunteered   14, 62, 69, 294, 318, 377, 441, 488, 506, 527, 575

volunteering   13, 33, 259

volunteering   option of   288

volunteers   13, 15, 25, 51, 279, 293, 297, 520, 545

vomit   pool of   26

vomit   reek of   26

vomited   511

vomiting   92, 241, 290, 315

vomits   26

voted   286, 326, 601

votes   597

vowels   33

vows   521

vulnerabilities   437

vulnerability   395

wa   42

wading   59

wafting   117

waged   482

wages   267

waging   479

wagons   22

wailing   201, 468, 510, 584, 585

wails   16, 216, 482

waited   142, 190, 211, 246, 276, 330, 511

waiting   4, 5, 12, 24, 26, 29, 36, 38, 44, 57, 79, 81, 82, 91, 104, 128, 141, 146,
151, 156, 159, 170, 173, 174, 176, 178, 181, 186, 196, 199, 204, 209, 212, 220, 227, 247, 256,

273, 274, 277, 280, 294, 318, 338, 340, 351, 372, 379, 386, 390, 399, 415, 425, 428, 433, 449, 453, 460, 463, 468, 469, 471, 485, 489, 491, 493, 496, 510, 511, 523, 528, 545, 551, 558, 561, 576, 589, 596, 603

waiting|I 461

waits 4, 9, 197, 220, 253, 302, 414, 421, 455, 594, 595

wakefulness 154

wakes 84, 156, 164, 171, 439, 494

waking 30, 165, 185, 249, 291, 333, 431, 481, 484, 561, 593

waking chatter of 180

walked 18, 57, 144, 172, 365, 403, 432, 470

walks 6, 21, 35, 46, 204, 255, 301, 303, 323, 334, 403, 430, 442, 463, 487, 517, 519, 538

wallowing 289

walls 24, 34, 35, 40, 46, 184, 239, 264, 265, 347, 406, 411, 415, 427, 447, 475, 482, 499, 503, 511, 551, 562, 563, 564

wandered 465

wanders 47, 109, 362, 463, 545, 562

wanly 479

want|what 399

wanted| 294

warbles 14

warded 504

warding 322, 338

wardrobes 185

warehouses 447, 453

warm mass of 356

warmer 23, 59, 171, 179, 380

warming 104, 122, 206, 267, 280

warms 84, 247, 259, 600

warned 190, 248, 427, 483, 490

warnings 156

warns 245, 254, 577

warped 341

warren's 517

warring 504

wars 424, 446

war's 602

was|an 501

washed 110, 160, 223, 364, 372, 434

washes 335

wasps 98, 99, 100, 101, 102

waste spirit of 430

wasted 217, 296, 324, 432, 474

watched 45, 54, 63, 164, 168, 193, 210, 222, 249, 270, 298, 320, 343, 404, 437, 474, 509, 518, 545, 588, 600 watches 127, 164, 191, 296, 379, 406, 544, 579

watching 17, 22, 29, 42, 44, 46, 52, 53, 56, 58, 59, 60, 83, 90, 93, 94, 98, 125, 129, 130, 135, 140, 148, 150, 158, 160, 165, 190, 192, 194, 195, 197, 208, 210, 211, 212, 220, 259, 261, 274, 282, 292, 294, 297, 298, 303, 304, 308, 310, 324, 330, 349, 350, 356, 365, 378, 381, 384, 394, 402, 403, 409, 410, 414, 422, 430, 436, 449, 458, 459, 469, 475, 478, 480, 484, 485, 515, 522, 524, 528, 545, 547, 551, 553, 554, 566, 580, 591, 597, 608

Watching Brutus 413

Watching Glimmer 102

watchtowers 227

water absence of 341

water bottles of 135

water canteen of 450

water circle of 362

water drips of 158

water gush of 559

water scarcity of 89

water| 88

waterbird 111

waterfalls 239

waters 159, 183

water's 132, 141, 168, 173, 350, 368, 387, 430

wavering 394, 479

waves 15, 69, 118, 175, 176, 221, 232, 316, 334, 335, 337, 338, 412, 448, 452, 454, 481, 510, 521, 522, 526, 538, 566, 569, 574

waving 30, 33, 84, 175, 193, 211, 219, 245, 305, 307, 450, 488, 499, 514

waxed 283

waylaid 499

weakened 446, 510

weakens 549

weaker 313

weaknesses 532, 535, 536

wealthier 20, 28, 51

wealthiest 16

weaning 403

weapon sort of 116

weapons 3, 24, 27, 51, 55, 60, 78, 79, 83, 85, 96, 97, 103, 105, 106, 107, 112, 125, 131, 138, 147, 166, 181, 182, 231, 232, 246, 254, 256, 272, 275, 285, 300, 305, 336, 337, 338, 340, 342, 343, 350, 358, 359, 360, 367, 368, 369, 371, 372, 397, 406, 410, 415, 418, 424, 429, 437, 438, 445, 452, 463, 470, 471, 499, 510, 531, 532, 536, 538, 545, 554, 568, 570, 579, 582, 583, 588, 589, 601

weapons| 274

wearing illusion of 187

wears 8, 42, 88, 193, 312, 315, 327, 418, 428, 436, 447, 457, 492, 508, 520, 567

wearying 571

weather's 154, 283

weaves   378, 481, 543

weaving   52, 64, 126, 200, 382, 540, 585

we'd   16, 20, 27, 37, 44, 45, 52, 61, 115, 130, 142, 157, 159, 202, 214, 215, 229, 258, 259, 263, 267, 301, 307, 314, 330, 412, 416, 420, 444, 468, 507, 508, 509, 515, 552, 571

wedding|but   328

wedges   369, 383

wedging   154

weeds   clump of   224, 225

weeks   6, 11, 16, 164, 191, 203, 210, 211, 238, 239, 266, 267, 282, 283, 293, 303, 316, 412, 425, 485, 492, 498, 504, 517, 518, 525, 576, 596, 600, 602

week's   409

weeps   567

weighed   224, 580

weighing   202, 290, 340, 382, 423

weighs   298, 326, 338, 385, 544

weightlifting   52

weights   50, 54, 133

welcomed   404, 405, 428

welcomes   249, 440

welcoming   228, 232, 308, 357, 577

we'll   4, 32, 35, 37, 48, 98, 108, 109, 111, 126, 129, 140, 141, 145, 149, 151, 161, 165, 167, 169, 170, 172, 174, 196, 200, 207, 228, 237, 249, 258, 266, 279, 295, 307, 324, 332, 333, 341, 344, 345, 358, 362, 370, 372, 382, 383, 385, 389, 417, 422, 425, 433, 439, 442, 443, 446, 451, 459, 479, 480, 484, 485, 497, 502, 505, 509, 510, 512, 524, 535, 538, 557, 577, 579, 596

Well|not   493

Well|we're   501

Well|yes   200

welts   94

were| 182

were|what   367

wets   306

wetting   350

What'd   44, 152, 505

What'd Peeta   530

Whatever I'm   158

Whatever Snow   562

whatever's   526

what's   13, 20, 31, 32, 33, 35, 38, 40, 42, 60, 61, 62, 68, 70, 71, 84, 86, 90, 95, 103, 111, 126, 133, 134, 136, 143, 151, 155, 156, 157, 168, 169, 177, 180, 185, 196, 197, 215, 225, 227, 232, 238, 241, 248, 251, 252, 265, 270, 271, 273, 278, 292, 298, 309, 312, 317, 340, 345, 348, 349, 356, 369, 382, 390, 392, 393, 407, 411, 418, 419, 422, 438, 443, 451, 452, 460, 461, 462, 463, 464, 472, 487, 501, 504, 506, 511, 513, 519, 520, 522, 523, 529, 530, 533, 535, 536, 542, 543, 545, 553, 560, 561, 564, 591, 592, 596, 600, 601

What's Peeta's   63

what's   reality of   565

wheedles		141
wheelbarrows		447
wheelchair's		456
where|I'm		241
where'd		60, 107, 269
Wherein Katniss		596
where's		85, 149, 151, 223
Where's Haymitch		24
Where's Peeta		264
Where's Portia		186
Where's Prim		476
Where's Volts		370
whimpering		179, 584
whimpers		478
whims	223	
whiner	34	
whipped		108, 260, 275, 297, 575
whipping's		108, 283
whips	374, 444, 461, 516, 561, 582	
whir	495	
whirls	152	
whisked		14, 37, 193, 577
whiskers		223, 569
whisks	284	
whispered		4, 143, 192, 491, 516
whispers		44, 53, 90, 124, 133, 138, 180, 186, 213, 241, 257, 274, 290, 359, 365, 376, 409, 418, 425, 435, 502, 514, 515, 516, 561, 563, 566, 607
whistled		168, 231
whistles		24, 168, 229, 230, 467
white pile of		280
whizzing		150, 336
who|who		157
who'd	25, 28, 258, 380, 405	
wholeheartedly		110
wholeness		412
who've		20, 303, 420, 456
Widening		503
widens		117
wider	209, 340, 345	
wielding		34, 174, 205, 314, 369, 585
wiggling		350, 483
wigs	567, 568, 579	
wild bed of		61
wild tops of		196
wildest		412

wildflowers 126, 196, 227

wildly 373

will| 15

willingness 116, 261

willows 83

wilted 486

win|I 163

winces 270, 594

wincing 72

windowpanes 262

windows 41, 47, 52, 77, 159, 184, 186, 196, 204, 227, 232, 243, 247, 266, 276, 324, 333, 397, 455, 514, 543, 546, 548, 551, 552, 570, 576, 580, 603, 604

window's 289

winds 261, 293, 349

wind's 44

wine offer of 41

wine smell of 72, 221

wineglasses 240, 321

winging 326

wings 68, 107, 232, 329, 344, 418, 433, 436, 438, 466, 498, 560, 585, 586, 593

winners 130, 227

winner's 191, 239

Winning|won't 70

winnings 229, 230, 233

wins 11, 34, 61, 108, 128, 153, 361, 417, 454, 515

winter dead of 238

winter's 479

wiped 71, 93, 167, 290

wipes 26, 64, 151, 205, 255, 301, 330, 527

wiping 22, 183, 275, 289, 317, 374, 409, 416, 546

wire coil of 368, 371, 402, 413

wire loops of 392

wire reel of 371

wired 383, 486

wires 183, 437, 510, 559

wire's 388

Wiress 315, 316, 317, 331, 339, 341, 345, 348, 349, 363, 364, 365, 366, 367, 368, 369, 370, 371, 378, 390

Wiress's 343, 366, 370, 371

Wish I'd 309, 588

wished 4, 60

wishes 46, 73, 242, 351

wishing 29, 75, 87, 125, 128, 260, 319, 420, 465, 466

Wishing Seneca Crane 260

wisps 355, 439

wistfully   324
withdrawing   358
withdraws   263, 414
withheld   162, 416, 506
withholding   90
witnessed   43, 335, 354, 562
witnesses   419, 432, 440
witnessing   245, 602
woes   125
wolfing   138
wolflike   261, 562
woman's   30, 279, 374, 567, 572
women   pair of   230
won| 287
wondered   17, 45, 276, 376
wonderfully   327
Wonderingly   328
wonders   50
won't   6, 7, 15, 19, 20, 22, 30, 36, 37, 41, 49, 63, 75, 79, 82, 83, 84, 87, 90, 93, 96, 113, 131, 132, 140, 141, 145, 146, 148, 151, 152, 156, 157, 158, 161, 163, 165, 166, 168, 173, 181, 182, 190, 191, 200, 217, 220, 226, 249, 250, 251, 252, 253, 257, 265, 269, 271, 284, 289, 290, 292, 295, 298, 313, 317, 323, 326, 327, 328, 332, 333, 346, 350, 358, 363, 368, 374, 377, 381, 388, 393, 399, 403, 406, 413, 415, 417, 422, 425, 443, 447, 450, 462, 465, 476, 480, 481, 483, 490, 495, 518, 519, 526, 527, 535, 537, 540, 549, 555, 556, 562, 570, 571, 573, 574, 575, 579, 589, 593, 595, 601, 602, 606, 608
wood   smell of   21
woods|but   14
wordlessly   42, 257
word's   505
words   list of   543
words| 329
workers   8, 174, 211, 268, 503, 509, 518
Workmen   558
workouts   531
world's   2
worms   2
worries   157, 177, 253, 322
worrying   216, 243, 271, 298, 325
worse   idea of   258
worsening   245
would've   104, 127, 163, 250, 256, 293, 406, 410, 443, 485, 486, 504, 517
wounded   hundreds of   455
wounds   105, 111, 122, 127, 133, 134, 140, 159, 195, 257, 302, 354, 355, 358, 359, 373, 375, 419
wracked   104

wrappings	205
wraps	19, 45, 65, 69, 154, 168, 266, 278, 279, 415, 419, 479, 513, 523, 568
Wreathing	126
wrecked	527
wrecks	454
wrenching	244, 329, 448, 546
wrested	410, 504
wrestled	189
wrestles	221
wriggles	160
wrings	257
wrinkles	67, 135, 204, 419
wrists	253, 255, 326, 389, 397, 399, 427, 470, 529, 560, 566, 568, 570, 571, 579
writes	369, 441, 536
writhing	363, 402, 548
wryly	204, 319, 414
www.suzannecollinsbooks.com	609
yanked	59, 223, 547
yanking	124, 146, 585
yanks	33, 151, 232, 372, 451, 483, 489, 565, 566, 585
yards	27, 52, 58, 59, 80, 84, 85, 91, 94, 112, 116, 137, 138, 145, 168, 169, 175, 188, 190, 224, 264, 267, 268, 272, 335, 336, 345, 346, 351, 352, 356, 357, 358, 370, 372, 386, 388, 392, 437, 439, 453, 454, 480, 485, 486, 537, 547, 564, 580, 598
yawns	561, 575
year's	8, 30, 73, 305, 320, 333, 350, 446, 507
Year's Day	52
years|some	191
yelled	29, 263, 468
yelling	8, 17, 62, 131, 145, 180, 185, 251, 414, 454, 468, 502, 547, 563
yellowed	247, 287, 288
yells	233, 509, 520
yes|for	597
yesterday's	222, 457
yields	511
yipping	176
York	1, 198, 401, 532, 609
York Times	609
York's	526
you|	161
you|handled	444
You|hung|Seneca Crane	322
you|in	473
you|lose	578
You|shoot	54
you|you	249

you'd 7, 42, 45, 72, 107, 108, 116, 132, 155, 159, 170, 224, 225, 228, 239, 240, 250, 260, 265, 280, 293, 301, 307, 313, 316, 322, 325, 328, 336, 357, 367, 398, 412, 423, 424, 431, 435, 437, 438, 462, 471, 483, 505, 507, 512, 517, 518, 542, 554, 555, 589

you'll 9, 20, 21, 28, 32, 36, 37, 49, 52, 62, 66, 113, 128, 135, 144, 145, 151, 155, 161, 169, 213, 219, 221, 234, 238, 240, 242, 249, 254, 273, 290, 322, 325, 332, 355, 360, 361, 368, 416, 423, 426, 429, 435, 438, 442, 443, 445, 450, 472, 502, 506, 508, 513, 530, 532, 537, 540, 557, 595

your|Annie 375

You're District Eleven 107

yourselves 74, 79

zapping 341

zippers 333

zips 14, 334

zones 383, 474, 567

9 781499 306064